Disclaimer

Madi's Prayer

Candace W Bookshelf Inc.
Publisher
All corporate inquiries can be sent to
admin@cwbooks.ca or
ccwells45@outlook.com

Written
by Candace C Wells Of
Calgary Alberta, Canada
www.cwbooks.ca

I am the creator of all characters, plot and settings of this book and it is fiction in nature.

The characters and settings are not affiliated with real places, events, or people.
I mention, Alberta and British Columbia only to indicate the Canadian
landscape and lifestyle and knowledge from my personal life.

The writings of this book may seem relative only to lifestyle as I have seen, heard,
and perceived over my years.

This story is written humbly to share the blessings of God when we choose his way
and not our way. I do not write to offend or hurt. Only, to recollect that we all make mistakes along the
way and there is a time to choose righteous living if we genuinely want to receive God's blessings.
There are consequences for our choices, right or wrong. Live and love through Christ's love and you
shall live.

All scripture is taken from the King James Version of the Holy Bible indicative of my
readings and my faith. It is written to indicate faith in God preserved in the characters
decisions and motivation for their life.

Regards

Candace C Wells

From the author –

To all my readers. I want to thank you for your interest in my first novel.
I hope you enjoyed the read. I ask that you try not to analyze the content
but can only see our hope is in trusting in Jesus Christ, every day for
everything that we need.

People all over this globe are in need, today, some more than others.

Always be careful to count every blessing that you have. Remember to live
and offer kindness everyday.

Let us pray;

Heavenly Father

*I thank you for your goodness. I ask you to bring each of us to a heart of forgiveness and purity and
lead us to your love and plan and purpose for each of us, today. Let's be careful not to judge nor to
boast.*

Prepare us for your coming day.

Let us all check our hearts. Remove every root of bitterness from our hearts that we may see you.

*Restore your people to your joy and restore the hearts of the parents to the children, and the children
to the parents.*

Thy will be done.

Amen

Madi's Prayer

Written by
Candace C Wells

One

It is a cold, mid-October morning in the Rocky Mountains. Madi leaves her home early to get across town to work. Madi is enthusiastic about the mountain and river valleys of British Columbia and Alberta. She has loved them since she was a little girl. Naturally, she makes her home in small town British Columbia, west of the Alberta border, in a place called Nucton. Nucton is a commercial logging town, full of rough men, saloons, and eateries, with a population of approximately fifteen thousand people. Madi is an avid skier. She works as a server at a local diner, Sam's Place. Liam purchased the diner from his father a year ago. Madi and Liam went through school together since Madi's third grade year. The job is a natural fit. Madi and Liam are like siblings. They have spent time together outside of work, not unusual to dinners, walks and hikes in the mountains. The places that require dates when you are single. You can say they are best friends.

Madi's work schedule runs around the lunch and dinner hour, and often into the evening. She likes her job. Her customers enjoy her sunny disposition. She is paid well to do it.

Her parents want more for her life. Madi is content. She does not want to bring them disappointment. She is unsure of what more she needs to do with her life, right now. Her dad would tell her how bright she is. He would tell her she is wasting her life with that Liam guy and the old diner. Her mother did not approve of Liam, either.

Madi wants to find God's plan for her life. She is not a bad person. She does good to others, every day. Madi is responsible with her life and makes good choices. Her school attendance was good. She received good grades in high school. She does what she believes to be right. She feels her parents have expectations of her that she cannot live up to, and her church the same. Madi feels at times to leave her church. She loves the people she grew up with. She knows her church locals are full of hypocrisy. Her friends do not want to attend her church. She wished she could change her church friends. They often condemn her for having friends outside of her religious circles. Madi is a strong, young woman. She is not afraid to stand alone, most days.

Madi has recurring dreams of her life and what she wants to do with it. She is not the girl that wants to be famous, or popular. Madi wants a quiet life among the outdoors in touch with nature and her maker. She wants someone to share her life with. She believes this will bring greater purpose into her life.

Madi often dreams about the cottage home in her future. There is a brook running behind the cottage. There is roughage, shrubs and grass and bright purple and yellow flowers that come out in full bloom, every spring. She believes that someone put this dream in her heart. Madi believes in the promises of God and all he asks is for us to obey him to have his blessings. The dream of the quiet, cottage life is an easy one to fulfill, she thought. The dream of the right partner is the difficult one. Madi continues to walk by faith and believe God to direct her path in life. Madi believes that prayer and choices bring about God's plan for each of us. Blessings come when we believe God and thank him for every good thing that comes to us.

Madi chooses to live and enjoy each day God gives her. She understands God's word. She prays and talks to God. She asks for his help. When Madi stumbles she gets up and keeps going.

The sin is giving up and not getting up again and moving forward with God's plan. She often hears the other women talking about other women and their failures in her own church. Madi knows it is wrong. This is the kind of stuff that makes Madi not want to be a part of the local church. Madi regains her strength each day to walk as God calls her every day.

Madi chooses to work where kindness matters.

"You are deep in thought, Madi," Liam says.

"What is on your mind? he asks. "Do you want to talk about something?"

"Not right now, Liam," Madi says. "I have to get back to work."

"Are you afraid I am going to tell your boss?" He asks with a giggle.

"I see you deep in thought a lot these days," Liam says. "You do not have to stay here."

"You can do more with your life, Madi," he replies.

"I know I can," she says. "I do not know what I should be doing."

"It seems there is so much pressure to do what others want me to do," she says.

"I want to choose my life," Madi replies. "And I want others to be happy for me."

"I hear you," Liam says. "It was a difficult decision to take over the diner from my dad when he fell ill."

"It felt the right thing to do," he says.

"It was all I knew," Liam replies. "I chose it, and I did it."

"Dad was going to sell the place," he says. "He did not think I had any interest in it."

"Now, this is my life until I choose to change it," Liam speaks.

"I enjoy talking to you, Liam," Madi replies. "You are wise beyond our years."

"It comes with running your own business," Liam replies. "You learn as you go."

"You have to do many different tasks," he replies.

"You hire and you fire," Liam says. "Every day is a new day."

"You do what you have to do," he says.

"You are smart," Liam says. "You will figure out what is right for you."

"Forget about what others think and say about you," Liam replies.

"I will say this again, religion is a stumbling block in your life," he continues. "Religion is an emotional tie in your life."

"I do not call myself a Christian, Madi," Liam continues. "It does not mean I do not believe, and I am without faith."

"The lunch rush will be in soon," he continues, changing the topic. "We need to get our work done."

"Thank you, Liam," Madi replies.

"Would you get the salad bar ready, Madi?" Liam asks. "I will grab the entrées."

"For sure, Liam," Madi replies. "I see customers coming, now."

"Yes," Liam says. "Coffee and tea are ready."

The lunch hour is always busy from eleven o'clock in the morning until two o'clock in the afternoon. Customers come and go until two-thirty. It gives Madi time to clean up before dinner and get a bite to eat herself. The cleanup is Madi's task. Liam does the operation stuff. The dinner rush starts arriving at four-thirty and ends around seven-thirty. The doors close at eight o'clock in the evening, most days.

Monday is Madi's day off, at the least. Madi works hard.

Madi is at home resting, on a Friday night after work. She curls up in her chair into a good book. She enjoys her own company, mostly. Maeve Binchy is one of Madi's favorite authors from her youth. Her favorite book, *"Light A Penny Candle,"* would move her to read for hours. It would make her laugh and cry. It is a definite original about friendship of two young girls socially not meant to be friends. Yet, they continue to be friends. Madi enjoys a good read when she can relate to the characters.

Madi answers her telephone. It is her mother calling.

"Hello," Madi says.

"Hello, Madi," mother replies. "Dad and I are checking up on you."

"I have been home from work for a couple of hours and had a bite of dinner," Madi replies. "I am enjoying my book."

"It has been a long week," Madi says. "I want to relax and enjoy my home."

"How is work?" mother asks.

"It is fine," Madi replies.

"I am happy for you," mother says. "We want what is best for you."

"I am happy," Madi replies. "It is enough for me."

"I love you, both," she says. "Good night, mom."

"Good night, Madi," mother says hanging up the telephone.

Madi continues to read her book for another half an hour. She retires to soak in a hot bath before bed to find relief for her aching feet.

She falls asleep as soon as her head hits the pillow. She does not stir all night.

Two

The sun rises, at six o'clock in the morning. It shines through her bedroom window. Madi can see the silhouette of the wrens on the front fence posts. They are chatting to each other and maintaining balance on the thin railing. Madi watches them from her dining room table as she eats breakfast. It makes her smile.

Liam decides it is time for Madi to take her holidays. School is in. The town is busy and back to work. Liam always has stuff for her to do.

Madi walks into work early, this morning. She left work from the night before.

Liam watches as she walks by his office.

"Hey, Madi stop by the office when you have a minute," he says.

"Sure," Madi replies. "I have a couple things to tidy up from last night."

Madi is responsible.

Liam can rely on her.

Liam is not looking forward to the day that Madi decides she is moving on.

"Hi," Madi says. "What's up?"

"When would you like to take your holidays?" Liam asks.

"You have three weeks paid vacation on the books," Liam says. "I need them cleared up before the end of the year."

"You have worked hard this year," Liam says. "I have a bonus for you."

"Thank you for all of your hard work, this year," Liam says handing her an envelope.

"Thank you, Liam!" Madi exclaims. Madi tucks the envelope in her right pocket. She will open it when she arrives home.

Liam looks up at Madi. "I would like you to take holidays over the next few weeks," Liam says.

"It will bring you back before the Christmas season."

"I have asked my sister Doris to cover for you," he replies. "It will not be the same without you, but we will be fine."

"I will tell her to be nice to your customers," Liam teases.

"Sure," Madi says. "I will have to figure out what to do with myself."

"Get away from this town," Liam replies. "You work so hard."

"I used to like to travel, alone," he says. "I am stuck here for now but that could change, too."

Madi does not know what that meant.

Liam can almost see her thoughts. "Madi, you can do better than this," he says.

"I am not going to be here, forever," he says. "I am thinking about selling the diner."

"I have some interest in buying the place," Liam replies. "I have not made my decision, yet."

"I, too, need to figure out what I want from life," he says.

Madi does not know what to say.

"Change is good," Liam replies.

"It was my father's business," he says.

"I have come a long way," Liam continues. "It has given me a good life"

"It is not my dream job," he says. "I am ready to let it go."

"I want to go back to school," Liam replies.

"To do what?" Madi asks.

"I have some ideas," he replies. "I will tell you more when you get back."

"As a friend, Madi," Liam says. "Get away from here and find your life."

"Come back and tell me all about it," Liam speaks. "I am still your best friend."

"I think I might do that," Madi replies. "I want to see San Diego."

Madi and Liam put the day in working together, talking often. They have been good companions since grade school. Madi often worries that Liam will find love, first.

The dinner hour is done. They are both tired and hungry. Madi tidies the kitchen, the tables, and the floors. Liam goes over the washrooms.

"You can head home now, Madi," Liam says. "I will finish up here."

"Thank you for all your help, Madi," he says. "Good night."

"Good night, Liam," Madi replies.

Madi makes her way to the door. She quietly sits behind the wheel of her car. She drives home that night deep in thought. She thinks on the envelope in her right pocket. She parks in her driveway and turns off the engine. She secures the club on her steering wheel. She grabs her coat and purse and heads into the house.

In the house, her shoes come off first. The epsom salt soak is calling her, tonight. She heads upstairs to turn on the tub and mix the salts. She stays with the tub. She reaches into her pocket and pulls out the envelope. She opens the envelope to find a letter from Liam, with a check attached. She reads the letter, first.

Dear Madi

You are the dearest friend that I have. Please accept this gift
as a token for all your hard work, standing beside me to the very end every night.

It is more than you expected. Business has been better than usual and
I recognize your efforts are a part of this. Please use it for yourself,
I am thinking a holiday or your education. I know you will use it towards
something good. When your vacation is over, please come by and tell me
all your good news and I will share mine.

Love Liam

Madi unfolds the check and reads five thousand dollars. She starts to cry. She does not know how to accept his gift. Madi will put it away in her savings account. She turns the water off. She tucks the letter and the check into her top dresser drawer.

Madi heads down the stairs to find her telephone. She dials Liam's number. His telephone rings twice. He answers on the third ring.

"Hello," Liam says.

"Hello," Madi replies. "Thank you, Liam!"

"I do not expect this," Madi says. "I enjoy every day we work together."

"You are my best friend," Madi replies. "You are so kind."

"If there is anything you need," Liam replies, "talk to me." "You are a beautiful woman."

"Good night, Madi," Liam says. "Get some rest!"

"Good night, Liam," Madi replies.

Madi tells no one. She will deposit it in the bank, tomorrow. She walks back upstairs to get into her cool bath. She runs the warm water into the tub to remove the chill. Madi lets her aching body soak for fifteen minutes before crawling into bed.

Madi falls asleep.

The sun shines through Madi's windows early in the morning. It startles her. She wakes up at six-thirty. It is Saturday. It is vacation time.

Madi has no reason to get up so early. She is rested. She rises and gets dressed.

She sits down and enjoys a cup of coffee, with a couple of slices of toast and raspberry jam. It is a beautiful, fall morning.

After breakfast, she slips on her red, rain parka with her purple sketchers. She is out the front door. Madi lives in a quiet, townhouse complex. There are bike paths behind her unit. She walks to the end unit to the north to follow the path down to the river.

Madi is entering her twenty-fourth year. It is time to think about her future.

Madi is a skilled young woman. She can do whatever she wants to do. Her heart wants to honor God with her choices and her life.

"Enough of these thoughts," she thinks to herself. *"Just enjoy the day and be thankful for each day."* "It will all work out."

Madi passes a goose on the pathway. She kneels to get close and talk to him. He is alone. This is strange. Usually, they travel together as mates. He looks up at her from one eye. His head is looking sideways to hear her voice. Madi looks at the goose. You have a great life. You have no cares or worries in this world. I want to live a simple life and be happy with my day-to-day decisions. It feels as if others want to make decisions for me.

Madi feels tears on her cheek, *"Oh, God, why does this bring me to tears."*

"I do not want to be like others," Madi thinks. *"I want to be me."*

Heavenly Father

Take the people from my life that want to steal my joy.
Forgive them and help them to find their life in you,
And help me to find my joy in you every day.

Amen

Madi heads home on the same path. She does not realize the distance she has walked. Madi feels it is time to see new see things, new scenes, and new people.

Three

On Monday morning, Madi books herself into a beautiful, ski resort, out of town. The place is surrounded with beautiful walking trails. There are horses and boats on the premises. There is no snow yet, so operations are still in place for the fall season. She is lucky enough to get a room for Friday night through until Sunday night.

Madi spends the morning organizing her home front. She enjoys getting caught up on her cleaning and laundry.

She plans to drive out Friday morning early by seven o'clock. She wants to arrive at the resort by eleven o'clock in the morning. Madi is excited. She needs the time alone. She looks forward to spending time with God and his word.

She cannot wait to ride a horse. Her day-to-day activities have become overwhelming. Madi makes herself a sandwich. She sits at the kitchen table with a glass of milk and quietly eats her lunch.

Heavenly Father

Please forgive me for trying to do everything myself.
I ask you to bring the changes in me you want to make
and take me to the place you want me to go.

Amen

Tears roll down Madi's cheeks, "*God give me strength each day to rely on you for new paths.*"

In quietness, Madi hears a voice behind her.

"*Be still and know that I am God.*" "*I will never leave you nor forsake you.*"

Heavenly Father

I thank you for your word.
I ask you to give me strength to endure
And obey your voice and to trust you for new paths.

Amen

Madi is encouraged to hear God's voice, so sure. She grabs her coat and shoes and heads outside for some fresh air. A walk will do her good, and a talk with the neighbors.

She remembers a scripture about God wanting to restore old paths. Her first thoughts, "*oh God, what do you want from me.*" "*I am more than able to make my own decisions,*" She knows better than to argue with God. The resistance only leads to rebellion. "*It is not always about the ability to make our own decisions.*" "*It is at times what God's love and mercy is trying to keep us from.*" "*God knows our days.*" "*He knows everything we need because he knows our future.*" Madi put the thoughts to rest.

Her neighbor, Ron, is in the front of his garage cleaning it out.

"Hello, Ron," Madi says. "How are you doing, today?"

"I am fine," Ron replies. "I need to get this place clean before the snow falls."

"You are not working, today?" Ron asks.

"No, there are some changes happening at the diner," Madi replies. "I am on vacation for a few weeks." "I cannot say too, much."

"I am not sure what is going on," Madi says. "I am off to the ski resort for the weekend for a time out."

"Have fun, Madi," Ron says. "It will all work out, be patient."

"Thank you, Ron," Madi replies. "The waiting is hard."

"We all like our comfort, Madi," Ron says.

"Welcome to the working world, kid," he states. "We have all been there."

Madi lived a protected childhood. All her decisions were made for. I suppose that is fine when you are kid. We all need to grow into an adult and learn to make our own choices. She does not want her parents making her decisions for her the rest of her life. She knows God's word as well as the others in church, although she attends irregular. She feels she can grow at home, reading God's word and listening to her own choice worship music. The music in the church she cannot relate to. It is empty. She is confident God knows her heart.

Heavenly Father

I know you hear my prayers.
You know exactly what I need.
I ask you to place in my path the things
I need to grow in you and prosper.

Amen

Madi arrives back home. She opens the front door and removes her coat and shoes. She tucks them away in the closet. She grabs her book and retires to her bedroom to read and rest. Madi knows God is calling her to rest. God has called Madi to live in relationship with him. She knows she is to wait on him for all good things.

Madi falls asleep.

Madi wakes up at one-thirty in the afternoon. She rolls over to look through the window. She feels rested. She is not ready to get out of bed. The telephone rings and it goes to voicemail. She does not want to talk, now. She reaches across to the night table to grab her book. She reads a page and moves to the next page, smiling and laughing. A good novel is a great way to lighten her heart.

Madi pulls herself up from her idle position. "*I better check my voicemail*," she thinks to herself. Madi grabs her telephone and heads down the stairs.

It is her mother. "*Hello, Madi just checking in,*" Madi listens. "*Hope everything is ok,*" "*Love mom and dad.*"

Madi dials her mothers' number. "Hello, mom," Madi says.

"Hello, Madi," mom replies.

"Sorry," Madi speaks. "I fell asleep after my walk."

"I have been house cleaning," Madi continues.

"I am on vacation for a few weeks," she says. "I am heading to the ski resort for the weekend."

"That is no place for a girl of your age, alone!" mother gasps.

"Mom, stop worrying," Madi says. "I will be fine!"

"I have always been careful where I go," Madi replies, "and what I do."

"We are praying for you, Madi," mom says.

"We love you," mom says. "Good night!"

"Good night, Mom," Madi replies. "My thoughts and prayers are with you always, love you." Madi heads upstairs and crawls back into her bed.

Madi falls asleep.

She wakes up to the birds singing and the sun on her face. She has the next two days to herself. It is eight o'clock in the morning. Madi has time to rest and enjoy the outdoors. She wants to be alone and spend her moments with God in nature.

"A long walk in the park down to the river will be good today," Madi thinks.

Tomorrow, Madi will give her girlfriend, Leah, a telephone call and have a lunch together.

Thursday she will be packing for the early, road trip on Friday.

Madi makes a cup of coffee. She adds a bit of milk. She has a banana for breakfast.

It is Wednesday, Madi dials Leah's number.

Leah picks up the telephone on the third ring.

"Hello, Madi," Leah replies. "It is nice to hear from you."

"It has been such a long time," Leah replies.

"I am sorry, Leah," Madi says. "You can call me, too."

"You work all the time, Madi." Leah says.

"That is real life, Leah," Madi replies.

"I am sure," Leah replies. "I love my life."

"I am getting married, soon," Leah says.

"I am happy for you, Leah," Madi says. "It is not what I want for my life, yet."

"It is choices, Madi," Leah replies.

"You are right," Madi says.

"I am on holidays for a few weeks." Madi continues. "I am heading out on Friday for a weekend getaway to the ski resort."

Leah does not have anything to talk about other than herself.

Madi stops the conversation.

"Take care, Leah, talk soon," Madi says.

Madi ties her running shoes. She puts her coat on over her shoulders. She shuts the door behind her. She can hear the birds singing. What a beautiful sound. She walks the path with the song behind her. It is like someone is trying to talk to her. It is a beautiful fall morning. The fallen leaves crackling under her feet. The sun and blue sky above her head and not a cloud above. She follows the bike path for hours. She walks far enough. It is time to head home. She heads back along the bike path seeing all the familiar homes, park benches, trees, and flowers. It passes quicker along the familiar ground. It is close to three o'clock in the afternoon when she arrives at her front door.

She is hungry. She does not have too much in the house. A tin of chicken noodle soup, crackers and cheese will have to do. She pulls a pot from her lower cabinet and opens the can. She adds the water and stirs it on the heat. She places crackers and cheese on a plate. She pours the soup into a mug and gently carries it to the table. She sips the soup and eats her crackers and cheese. She is enjoying the moment in quietness. One person at a time is enough for Madi. Madi is a thinker and finds herself often talking to

God. She picks up her dishes and places them in the sink.

"It is time to stretch out and finish her book," Madi thinks to herself. She picks up the novel from her side table. She sits back into the comfort of her front room chair. She turns the light on beside her, adjusting the dimmer. She turns the pages, laughing to herself as she embraces the characters of the story. She is into her book and hours pass. Her stomach is telling her that it is dinner time. There is not much in the house to eat. Madi does not want to pick up groceries. She is packing tomorrow and will be driving out for the weekend on Friday morning. She decides on Sam's to have a burger with Liam.

Madi locks the front door with her jacket on her arm. The evenings are often cool around here. She tucks herself behind the wheel of her car. She starts the engine and backs out of her driveway. The music is quiet in the background. She can hear it enough to help her hold the tune as she sings along. It is only a fifteen-minute drive to the diner. She parks the car. She grabs her purse and walks to the front door. She locks the doors leaving her jacket behind the seat.

Liam sees her and greets her with smile. "It is nice to see you," he says.

"It is nice to see you, too," Madi says. "What is for dinner?"

"I am hungry," she replies.

"Doris is running a couple of family favorites as specials," he says.

"Sounds good," Madi says. "I will go in and have a look."

Madi looks over the dinner specials. Nothing there seems to delight her. She reaches for the regular menu. Madi settles on the original, Sam's burger. It is her favorite, the way that Liam makes it. He is careful in everything he does. He takes pride in every plate he serves. Madi orders her original burger, with white cheddar. She smiles at Doris, and Doris smiles back at her. It is as if she knows something. Madi does not know much about Doris. She is Liam's eldest sister, seven years Madi's senior. Bella is the next sister. She is five years Madi's senior. Madi spends her time at the diner and with Liam on extracurricular events. His sister's lives never become a part of their lives.

It is not long before Doris arrives with Madi's burger. The greens are fresh with a little bit of vinegar and oil the way Madi likes them. She is hungry. It is getting late. She wraps up the leftovers, pays the bill and heads out the door. Tomorrow will come early. She wants to get on the road before the sunrise. Madi wants to get to bed early. She arrives home at eight-thirty. She grabs her stuff from the car and locks the door behind her. She opens her front door. She drops her things on the floor and unties her shoes. She slips her shoes from her tired feet.

Madi puts the leftover dinner in the fridge. It will be a nice lunch for the road trip.

Madi heads upstairs to the bedroom. She slips out of her clothes and drapes a cool, summer night gown over her head and shoulders. She brushes and flosses her teeth. Her bags are packed outside the bedroom door ready for her last-minute supplies. At last, Madi is ready. The alarm is set for five o'clock in the morning. Madi tucks herself into her bed and is soon asleep.

The alarm rings at five o'clock as expected. Madi jumps from her bed. The warm shower feels good on her back and then on her face. It helps to wake her. She washes her face and grabs a towel to wipe the water from her body. Madi brushes her teeth and runs her fingers through her hair. She grabs a ball cap for her head. It will have to do for the morning journey. Madi grabs her last-minute things stuffing them in the bag where they will fit. She grabs her lunch. She ties her shoes and locks the door behind her. Her bags are in the car trunk. She is off. Madi stops at McDonalds to grab a coffee on her way out of town.

Her favorite radio station is playing softly. It is a lovely morning. Madi is singing, sipping coffee and her GPS is filling her in with every direction to start her trip. Her drive time is four and a half hours. Madi will arrive sometime between ten-thirty and eleven o'clock this morning, at her favorite resort.

It is a beautiful drive along the highway east of Nucton along the mountainside. The rich, lush green hills and the creeks running off the mountains, down the banks of the roadside are splendid. Madi plans to drive and stop half-way. She will have her lunch at a picnic area, along the way. Madi drives for two and a half hours. She can feel her stomach growling. Her coffee cup is empty. She knows she will need a refill at the next service station for coffee and fuel.

Madi sees a Shell station up ahead. It is time to pull off the road and do what she needs to do. She pulls her car up to the pump. She puts in another thirty dollars. It will carry her in her small sedan. She uses the washroom. She grabs a large, black tea and cream, inside the store. She closes the lid tight. She notices a picnic table on the way. She parks her car and grabs her bag lunch and tea. Madi enjoys the time out of the car and a bite to eat. She walks a stretch for her tired legs after lunch. She heads back to the car to make the last leg of the trip.

Four

Madi can see the gate posts of the resort. She made it. She is excited. It is going to be a great weekend. She is right on time. Madi pulls the car up into the driveway. The scenery with the mountains and waterscape is beautiful. Madi is going to enjoy the photography out here, the horseback riding and canoeing. She grabs her bags from the back seat. She does a final check of the backseat. She locks her car doors and walks up to the font doors.

"Hello, my name is Madison Leer," she greets the staff.

"I have a reservation for three nights," Madi says. "I am checking out Monday morning."

"My telephone number is (604)27X-3X29."

"Thank you," the lady replies at the counter. "I have you booked into room 312."

"May I see a credit card and your driver's license?" the lady asks.

Madi pulls her identification from her wallet and hands it to the lady.

The lady is quick to go through all the processes with her. She hands Madi back her identification after running her credit card through the machine.

Madi accepts the receipt.

The lady hands her the key and directs her to her suite.

Madi opens the door to her room. It is the same as she remembers. A queen size bed to the right of the room across from a full three-piece bath. A sofa across from the TV where she can relax. A microwave and a fridge where she can keep snacks when she wants to be alone.

"What a haven of rest," she thinks to herself.

Madi unpacks her bags and puts her things into the bedroom closet. She does not enjoy living from a suitcase. She likes her comfort and feeling at home. She finds a fresh pair of walking shorts and a t-shirt. She enjoys a nice, warm shower to wash away the travel dust. She turns the water off and grabs a towel. She dries her body and wraps the towel around her head. Madi steps outside of the bathroom to find her clothes. She slips into her clean clothes. Madi feels great. She grabs her room key and tucks it inside her purse. She ties her shoes and leaves the room closing the door behind her. It is such a beautiful day to walk the grounds. Madi is off to become familiar with the lifestyle and meet the staff.

Madi walks along the trails. The trails travel for miles around the lake, passing the horse corrals and the barns. She passes the boat house, too. It brings back old memories. Madi would come out after her high school years with friends during the summer. Her friends have moved on with their lives. They have married and some have even moved out of Nucton. Madi got lost in the work world. Liam remains her closest friend. They share most everything. She often wonders if it could be love.

"Could it be enough to hold them together for the rest of their life?" She pushes the thoughts aside. Her parents would never approve. Madi often wonders if it matters who you love if you are true and honest with one other. She knows the biblical virtues of love and the promises that come with good and right choices. Madi knows these promises are to protect her. She believes that love is a commandment and therefore a choice for us to live every day. The scripture teaches us not to be unequally yoked with an unbeliever. She knows the wrong man will complicate her walk with God. Madi knows Liam is not right for her. He needs to come to the knowledge of Christ's love for his life. Madi continues to pray every day for her best friend Liam. She wants him to come to the knowledge of her faith in God. Madi does love Liam. Madi knows the day will come to surrender him over to the will of God.

It is a beautiful walk. It is hot for an autumn day with a cool breeze. Madi sings from her heart. It is a hymn she used to sing in church. It fills her heart with God's love. The words fill her mouth with praise to God. It rings a sweet, rich fragrance in her ears. Madi loves to give thanks to God every day for the good things God has done in her life, today and yesterday.

Madi has no idea of her future. She is going to wait on God and enjoy each day. She likes her job. She loves the people she serves. Madi does not like it when other people speak thoughts in her head.

Madi passes the boat house, she passes the barns, and she stops to talk to the trail guide.

"Hello," Madi says to the guide. "I would like to go on a trail ride tomorrow, afternoon."

"Book it at the front desk," the guide replies. "If you do not mind you could tag along with another group."

"That will be fine," Madi replies walking up the pathway to the hotel. She books the trail ride for one o'clock, the next day.

"It is close to lunch time," Madi says to herself, *"maybe I should stop for a small bite."* Madi sits down in the shade of a two-seat table on the patio. She orders a glass of water and a bowl of soup with a half of a roast beef on rye sandwich. Madi likes the resort. She feels free away from her regular routine. The staff are friendly. She enjoys their companionship during the work hours. She visits the staff in the guest facilities after their work hours. Madi makes new friends wherever she goes. Her friends come and go and only a handful remain in her life.

Madi walks down towards the boat house. It is a nice afternoon to get on the boat. The waves and water often calm her. The sunshine on her body feels warm upon her body. The man at the boat house asks Madi if she would like to go on the water. He startles Madi. She did not see anyone around. She looks around and sees a handsome young man standing in front of her.

"Hello, my name is Jake," he says. "I did not mean to startle you."

"I did not see you," she replies. "I was daydreaming."

"Yes," Madi says. "I would like to get out on the water."

"I am down for the weekend and heading home on Monday morning," Madi says. "I am on a trail ride, tomorrow afternoon, and relaxing all day Sunday."

"I get it," Jake replies, "the pressures of life and growing up."

"I am here because I want to be," Jake replies. "I enjoy what I do."

"I like what I do to," Madi replies. "I wish others would accept me for that."

"I understand, Madi," Jake replies. "Society has put an image on people they think to be right."

"Somehow, the church has tried to adopt the ways of the world to make us acceptable to the world, Madi," Jakes says.

"Those of us that know right need to continue in prayer," Jake says. "We need to always be in love and lead God's people back into the right."

"We need to trust in God's word and seek him for what is right for our own life, too, "Jake says.

"You are so wise, Jake," Madi replies. "I know I think too much of what others think of me."

"It is all normal," Jake replies. "Find your happiness in God's love and let it be enough."

"When you experience God's love," Jake replies. "It is enough." "And then it does not matter what others think of you because you live to please God."

"He will always bless his ways," Jake says. "Independence is not something to feel shame about even as a young woman." "If marriage is meant to be it will come to you."

"Get on the boat," Jakes insists. "Let's go for a ride."

Madi steps onto the boat. Jake hands her a life jacket. She places it around herself and buckles it up snug. Madi likes to play it safe. Jake puts the boat in gear and takes it to the middle of the lake. Madi sits on the side of the back bench. Jake gears the boat up, the way he likes to on a usual hot afternoon. They enjoy the cool back splash from the waves he creates. They both giggle as the waves splash over and onto them. Madi enjoys the laughter, the sunshine and the new friendship beginning. Madi let go of the pressures of life for the moment.

Jake docks the boat at the boat house.

The time passes and dinnertime arrives. It is a cool walk back to the hotel. Madi heads upstairs to her room. She freshens up for the evening. She finds something clean to wear to dinner. She slips into a pink summer dress. She sits down and enjoys a cup of tea. She reads a couple of chapters in her book. She heads downstairs to dinner.

The dining room is near empty by the time Madi arrives. It is less than a third capacity. She takes a table in the southwest corner of the room. She sits a little way from the exit. The server leaves a menu after pouring her a glass of ice water. Madi ponders the menu. She decides on a seafood dish. The baked cod with rice pilaf and the salad bar is perfect. It arrives minutes after she closes the menu. Madi knows her serving etiquette.

Madi places her order and walks up to the salad bar. She finds a lovely selection of fresh fruits and vegetables; tossed salad with tomatoes, onions and croutons, a touch of cheddar cheese drizzled with a little Italian dressing. She decorates her plate with cantaloupe and melons. Madi sits down and places her napkin on her lap. She eats her salad. She finishes the salad, and the cod dish arrives, topped with a tomato gravy and herbs. It is lovely. Madi finishes the meal. She pays the bill and heads up to her room.

Later that evening, Madi is in her evening attire. She stretches out on the sofa with her book and a cup of green tea. It is a nice evening drink before bed. Madi runs through the TV channels to see if any interesting movie might intrigue her. She surfs through the channels a couple of times and nothing. She shuts the TV off and returns to her book. The evening approaches ten-thirty, her eyes are heavy. It is time to call it a night. She tucks herself into the queen size bed under the comforter. She is soon asleep.

Morning wakes early with the sun shining through the window at six o'clock in the morning. Madi is not ready to get up. It is vacation time, but the day is telling her it is time to rise. She rolls over to face the other direction. Madi likes the mornings. This morning she wants to sleep. She has a trail ride at one o'clock with nothing else on her agenda today. She lay there in bed for another hour. She wakes up at seven-thirty.

Madi makes herself a cup of coffee. Madi sips her coffee, sitting on the sofa with her feet up still in her pyjamas. She is in no rush to go anywhere. She is not hungry. Madi does not like to overeat. She is careful with her weight.

Madi finds bath salts tucked in the drawer. She slips into the tub. Madi relaxes in a warm tub for an hour. She lays back, closes her eyes, and enjoys the warmth of the water around her body.

Madi falls sleep in the tub. She startles herself. It is time to get out, her fingers and toes are wrinkled. She reaches for her towel. She does a pat dry down her body and wraps the towel around the crown of her head.

Madi's clothes are set out on the bed in the other room. She dresses herself, slowly. The towel slips off her head and falls to the floor. Her wet, limp hair falls onto her shoulders. Madi runs her fingers through her hair. It is all she does with her hair most mornings.

Madi's clock reads ten forty-five. She had no idea. She enjoys the moment. Madi does a quick tidy of the room. She heads out to grab a bite to eat before leaving to catch up with her trail ride.

The deli is full of great sandwich selections and vegetables trays. She grabs herself a tuna sandwich and a vegetable tray, with a glass of milk. Madi finds a table away from the hot sun. She sits in the cool and enjoys her lunch. She can see the barns from her table. It looks like Jake is tending to the horses. She hopes that Jake will join them on the ride. Madi likes their conversation. She wraps up her lunch excess and tosses the wastage in the garbage. She wipes her hands and sanitizes on the way out of the door.

Madi catches herself singing that familiar hymn as she walks the path to the barns. She is happy.

Madi feels new in her life. There is a joy welling up inside her heart. She is at peace in her moment. Madi can feel God's presence beside her. She knows everything is going to turn out all right. Her faith and love for God will never fail. She arrives at the barns. Jake looks at her.

"Good morning, Madi," Jake says. "You look great this morning."

"Thank you, Jake," Madi replies.

"Yes, Madi, I am the trail guide this afternoon," Jake replies.

"The horses are my first love," Jake says. "I picked out this little gray, appaloosa for you,"

"He is a gentle, gelding."

"What are you wearing for shoes?" Jake asks. "It is always best to have a little heel to ride in the stirrup."

"Ride with your weight on your toes, please," Jake says. "We keep our trail rides to a walk as we ride mostly with inexperienced riders."

Madi is fine with this. She has no plans to race with horses she does not know. Horses are powerful creatures and can take a mind of their own with inexperienced riders.

"There will be five of us plus myself going out this afternoon," Jake says. "I will be your lead."

"Please do not get ahead of me."

Madi likes the confidence Jake displays as he sits on his mare. Madi does not ride enough to share the same. Madi has respect for the horse. She does as Jake says.

"We will be going around the lake, today," Jake says. "I want to get as close to the walking trail as we can."

"We will get close to the base of the mountain," Jake replies.

"We may go through some muddy waters." Jake says. "Let's keep out of the brush and branches."

"Have some fun and relax," Jake speaks. "Enjoy your ride, today."

Madi's horse is Pete. He is a beautiful dapple, gray color with not much of a tail. It is particular to the appaloosa horse. He has a nice stance and walks with grace even for his size. Madi is glad to be a part of the trail ride. They will be on the trail for a couple of hours. It will be long enough for any inexperienced rider. They arrive at the water ford where the horses need to cross. They stop and let the horses drink their fill. It is a beautiful ride and is soon time to turn back and head home.

Madi can see the barns. She is ready to be back. She is hot, tired, and full of horsehair. The horses all arrive at the barns. Madi slips off the side of her horse. She knows enough to mount and unmount the horse, correct. Jake grabs the reins from her. Madi thanks him. She heads back to her room. Madi needs to shower and wipe off the dust before dinner.

Jake removes the saddles and brushes down the horses. He waters the horses before putting them out to pasture. Jake thoughts are toward Madi. She is such a nice girl. He hopes to get to know her more. Their lives are miles apart. He hopes their paths will cross again. Tomorrow is a busy day for Jake. It will be difficult to see her. He knows Madi is leaving early Monday, morning. Jake returns his thoughts to the barns. He puts the saddles and tack away. Jake heads up to his own room and relaxes.

Five

Madi is sitting in the dining room. Her dinner arrives. Madi's fork is in her hand when she feels something behind her. She turns around to see Jake standing there.

"Hello, Madi, may I join you?" Jake asks.

"That is fine!" Madi replies.

Jake puts his dinner tray on the place setting across from Madi. "Eating alone deserves a break occasionally," he says with a tease. "I am glad I found you here."

"The chances were good," he chuckles to himself. "I want to get to know you more."

"Thank you, Jake," Madi replies. Madi stops to enjoy her dinner. She smiles back at Jake. He too, is enjoying his dinner.

"You clean up very well, Madi," Jake says looking up at her.

"Thank you," Madi blushes.

"This is how I always look," she thinks to herself. Madi likes to be tidy when she is out in public. It is proper. Madi does not receive too many compliments, nor does she look for them.

"I would love to get to know you, Madi," Jake says. "Where are you from?"

"I grew up in the town of Nucton," she replies.

"I work for a local diner, or worked, for one," Madi says. "I enjoy what I do but everyone thinks I am wasting my life."

"I pay my bills," she replies. "I smile most every day."

"I love God," she says, "and I love to sing and praise his name."

"What more do I need?" she asks. "I will be twenty-five this year."

"I am twenty-six," Jake replies. "That sounds like a full life."

"It is," Madi replies.

"I grew up in a complicated church," she speaks. "It seems that everyone is in each other's business more than their own."

"I understand," Jake says, "that is a people problem and a sin problem."

"Jesus never did approve of it in his house," he says. "He will correct all things in good time."

"You have to learn to walk away and leave these things with God," Jake continues. "We must always be forgiving because we sin, too."

"God dwells in the hearts of his believers," Jake says, "not in the organized religion."

"People are complicated all over the globe, Madi," Jake continues.

"Mostly because of poor choices and sin."

"We need to learn how to protect our hearts," Jakes says. "And keep our own lives clean from the things of this world including the idols in religious, bureaucracy."

"I have been alone most of my life," Madi speaks. "Liam is my best friend."

"He is not a Christian and does not profess his faith as such," Madi says. "I love him, but I cannot marry him."

"God knows the countless hours I have prayed he would see the way I believe, and nothing changes," Madi replies. "I just stopped praying."

"That is the right thing to do," Jake says. "You are trying too hard to make the will of God happen."

"Let it go and God will bring every right in your life."

"I have been at the diner since I was seventeen," Madi continues. "Liam asked me to take my vacation up until Christmas."

"He handed me my bonus," Madi replies. "He is making changes, and I may not have a job to go back to."

"Just leave it alone," Jake replies. "God knows what you need."

"Good night, Madi," Jake says.

"Good night, Jake," Madi says. "It was a good time." Madi leaves the dining room. She heads up the stairs to her room. She had a great weekend and enjoyed meeting Jake. The social time intrigued her at the resort. She did not find time alone with God as she had hoped. She found exactly what she did need for the moment.

The time is nine-thirty. It is not late. Madi has all day tomorrow to walk the grounds. She steps into the shower. She slips into her summer, night gown. Madi soon stretches out on the sofa into her book. She turns the TV on to see if any movie showing might intrigue her. She searches to find a good drama not too much on the sappy side. She settles on Kate and Leopold, A little sappy. It was really all that was playing. Madi has not seen it in forever. It is funny and charming as Hugh Jackman and Meg Ryan are in their respective roles. Madi thought it cute for the moment. She turns off the TV.

Madi wakes up the next morning in a hot, hotel room. The sun is shining bright through her window. She slept in. Madi tidies her belongings to prepare for the early morning outing on Monday. She jumps into the shower and throws her clothes on and brushes her teeth.

Madi heads downstairs to get breakfast. She is hungry. Madi arrives at the dining room to find it filling up, fast. Jake is in the corner finishing his breakfast. She turns her head not to notice him. She wants to be alone, today. Madi finds a table in the opposite corner and the server seats her. He pours her a glass of water.

The server hands her a menu. Madi knows what she wants to eat. The server arrives in just minutes. He looks at her with a smile. "Are you ready to order?" he asks.

"Yes, please I would like bacon and eggs, eggs over easy and a slice of your multi grain toast with butter," Madi replies.

"A cup of coffee would be great." Madi smiles.

"Sounds good," he says. "A young lady that knows what she likes."

"Yes," she replies. "I like to make decisions."

"These skills are important, in life," the server replies.

"Yes," she says. "I must eat."

"I have some important decisions to make soon," she replies with a smile.

"All the best to you," he replies. "I am sure you will be fine." The server leaves her table after pouring Madi a cup of coffee.

Madi eats her breakfast. She is anxious to get on the grounds for a long walk alone with God. She had a wonderful time with the people around the grounds. It will be time to go home, soon.

Madi takes the trail to the immediate right of the hotel. She knows where it leads, right down to the water at the base of the mountain. She is not walking that far today. It is the opposite direction where the trail ride went the other day. She guesses it to be about a four-hour walk. The time is eleven o'clock in the morning. She will arrive back around three or three-thirty. It will be a wonderful way to wind up her weekend. She will arrive back to her room and have a nice shower. And enjoy a bite to eat in the dining room for her last evening. She looks forward to a good night's sleep, tonight.

Madi ventures out on the long trail ahead. She takes in the scenery. The evergreens are her favorite. The dark green from the top to the bottom intrigued her thoughts. The balm trees are beautiful with their arms and crisp leaves, but not to match the evergreens. They enveloped a warm feeling around her, kind of a comfort to walk in.

Madi is always careful to make a noise when she walks and sticks to the trail. She sings along the way. Madi often expects to be alone on the trail. She passes more people coming and going than normal. She says a quick hello on the way by. Madi calculates her distance to be about an hour from the lake. She walks to the lake front and turns back.

Madi enjoys each stride as it comes. Jesus taught in the Bible to occupy until the end. He gave each of us the ability to choose. Wisdom comes from learning. Occupy is a choice he gave each of us to make. It is something we need to determine based upon our own personal need. Madi is not prepared to step into any level of education at this time. It does not make sense. Madi will talk more with Liam about this. She decides to remain on staff at Sam's or pursue other employment even it meant moving to another town or city. She knows Nucton. There is not another diner she feels comfortable to work for. Madi makes her decision. She knows it will work out for her good.

Madi does not realize how far she has walked. She is hot, tired, and hungry. She is relieved to have come back into her reality. Her heart is full of joy. She feels like leaping. She does not want to go to school. She is good with her decision. Madi can hear a song in her heart and mind. She sings out. Madi does not care what people around her think. She is not harming anyone, at the least. She is praising and singing to her God with thanksgiving in her heart. God has heard her prayer. Madi arrives back at the resort at two-thirty in the afternoon. She unlocks the door to her room. She steps into a warm shower. Madi puts on a clean pair of walking shorts and a t-shirt. She prepares her room for a quick exit early in the morning. Madi will follow the same route home. She will stop only to fuel the car and fill her coffee mug.

Six

Madi wakes to the sound of her alarm at five o'clock the next morning. She jumps in the shower. She dries her body and puts on the same clean walking shorts and t-shirt. She does a quick check of the room. She grabs her backpack and heads out of the door. Madi pays her final bill. She thanks the staff for a lovely time.

Madi receives the cordial handshake. The staff are happy to see her.

Madi had a lovely time. She puts her backpack in the backseat of the car. She lay her jacket over the top of her bag. Madi jumps in the front seat, turns on the ignition and adjusts the radio volume. Madi is on the road, just a little before five-thirty. She is singing to the radio tunes. Madi is attentive to most genres. She has never been a fan of rock. Mostly, she likes to praise and lift God up in song. There are times when she likes a little country, a little pop, a little folk until it gets to be sappy and teary. It is time to change the station. Madi likes her simple life. She has no favorite stars. Madi is black and white. It is not the way Madi likes it to be, it is what she knows to be true by what she reads in God's word. She works hard and on her own time, she enjoys peace.

Madi does not enjoy the company of a crowd. She enjoys her one-on-one social moments. She never had a best friend, until Liam. She tries hard to be nice to everyone, even when it is difficult at times. Madi longs for the right one to share her life with.

The drive went by quickly with Madi deep in thought. She stops at the service station. Madi fills her sedan and her coffee mug. She grabs a snack for the last leg of the trip home.

Madi will be home for brunch.

The time is ten-thirty. Madi pulls into her driveway. It is good to be home. Madi has made a nice little nest for herself. She grabs her bag and jacket from the backseat and locks the car. Madi walks up to her front door. She puts her key into the key slot.

"Hello, Madi," Ron speaks.

"Welcome home," Ron says. "I hope your trip went well."

"It did," Madi replies. "Thank you."

"It went really, well," Madi says. "I met some good people."

"I felt some good prayers and made some new decisions," she says.

"I am happy for you, Madi," Ron replies.

"You are a bright girl," he says. "I have watched you grow for many years."

"I knew your parents when you were young," Ron says. "You always had spunk and a mind of your own."

"Thank you, Ron," Madi says.

"I do what I have to do," she says. "I have probably lost a few friends along the way."

"Do not worry what others think," Ron replies. "Walk where you feel led."

"You are going to be alright," Ron says.

"Thank you, Ron," Madi replies.

Madi and Ron say goodbye at the front door.

Madi steps inside, closing the door behind her. She slips off her shoes and drops her bag on her bed emptying all its contents. The laundry went into the basket and the toiletries into the bathroom to put away later. It was a short trip. There was not much to clean up after.

Madi does need to go to the grocery store. She would deal with that tomorrow. Madi wants to call her parents. She would then slip down to Sam's for a late lunch and say hello. Madi wants to see Liam.

Madi dials her mothers' number.

"Hello," mother says.

"Hello, mom," she speaks, "Madi here." "I just want to let you know I am home."

"Thank God, you called!" mom exclaims. "We were worried!"

"I told you I would be fine and that I would call when I got home," Madi replies. "I just got in the door here."

"I had a quick chat with Ron across the street and stepped into the house," she explains.

"I am glad you did," mom says. "Thank you."

"We love you," mom says. "Come for dinner one night this week."

"Sure," Madi replies, "maybe tomorrow night."

"That will be fine," mom replies.

"I am going to run out in a bit and grab a bite to eat," Madi says. "I need to get groceries in the house."

"I will see you tomorrow," Madi says.

"Is four o'clock, ok?" Madi asks.

"That sounds fine," mom replies.

Madi grabs her purse, slips on her sneakers, and heads out the door. She locks the door behind her. Madi backs her car out of the driveway. She heads off to the diner. She waves at Ron, and he waves back. Ron is like a father to Madi.

Madi pulls up in her usual parking stall at the diner. She steps inside the entrance of the diner.

Liam greets her with a smile. "Good to see you," Liam says.

"It is good to be home," Madi replies.

"I thought I would stop by for some lunch," Madi says.

"I am hungry," she replies. "I hope you have a nice soup and sandwich for me."

"Always for you Madi," Liam says. "It is on the house, today."

"Awe, thank you, Liam," Madi says. "I just got home this morning and called my parents."

"I unpacked and headed up this way," she replies.

"I am glad that you did," Liam says. "Doris and I have been doing some talking, lately."

"We are making some changes around here," Liam continues. "We want to discuss it with you."

"You are a definite asset to us," Liam speaks. "We have an offer for you."

"Enjoy your vacation and come by on Friday," Liam says. "We will sit down and discuss it."

Madi is happy. "Thank you, Liam!" Madi exclaims. Madi has nothing else to say. She knows it is an answer to her prayer.

"It is our pleasure," Liam replies.

"Madi," Liam speaks.

"You do not have to hide your faith," Liam says. "I am a believer, too."

"It may not be doctrine for doctrine," Liam replies. "I am sure that God will forgive me."

"I have done a lot of thinking with you away," Liam says.

"I really missed you, Madi," Liam continues with a smile. "I love you."

"I love you, too." Madi says. "We have been foolish not to discuss it sooner."

"I hope your parents will learn to accept me," Liam replies.

Madi does not know what to say. Her soup and sandwich arrive at her table. She has an excuse for quietness now. Madi adds a little salt and pepper and a touch of butter to her cream of broccoli soup. Madi has tears in her eyes. She does not know what to say. She was not prepared for all of this. They will need to talk. He has been silent for so many years.

"*What is he thinking*? "Madi asks herself, "*Why did he wait so long to tell me*?" Madi does not want to judge him. She will wait for Friday and see what it brings. Hopefully, before long she and Liam can have a heart to heart and discuss their personal lives.

Madi finishes her lunch.

Madi and Liam say goodbye. "When did you want to talk more about this, Liam?" Madi asks.

"I am hoping I can take you out for dinner on Saturday night?" Liam asks.

"That is fine," Madi says.

"You can come by my place for dinner." she says.

"I want to take you some place nice, for this moment, Madi," Liam replies. "I can pick you up at six-thirty."

"Alright, I will be ready," Madi smiles walking out the door. Madi's drive home is a quiet one. She arrives home and parks her car. She steps in the house locking the door behind her. Madi heads upstairs. The afternoon is still young and Madi is exhausted with all the excitement.

She falls asleep on her bed.

Seven

Madi wakes up with a startle at eleven-thirty in the evening. She is hungry. She has been asleep since five o'clock in the afternoon. There is nothing to eat in the house. She had plans to get groceries in the morning. She is going to have to run to the corner store to satisfy her stomach. Madi wants a cup of coffee. She chuckles to herself. She is feeling like a schoolchild. She puts on a t-shirt and a pair of loose-fitted pants. Madi slips on her fall jacket, the nights are cool, now. She puts her sneakers on and grabs her purse and keys.

Madi closes the door behind her. She leaves the door unlocked. She will be right back. The neighborhood is quiet. She feels safe. She drives the car down to the Esso station. Madi makes herself a cup of fresh mocha with cream. She finds nothing appetizing at the deli counter. She grabs a bag of cheezies and licorice. Madi grabs a small container of milk for her cereal in the morning. She will pick up groceries right after breakfast.

She will be at her parents for dinner, later that evening. It will be fun. She hopes.

Madi gets in her car and drives back to the house. She puts the milk in the fridge, taking her mocha and munchies, up to her bedroom. Madi turns the lamp light on, shutting the other lights off behind her. She sits up in bed sipping her warm mocha and enjoying each bite of the cheezie. It is close to midnight. The mocha is warm. She enjoys every sip until the cup is empty.

Madi is getting sleepy. She throws the mocha cup in the trash can. She slips into her night gown, and crawls under her sheets. She rolls over and turns the bed side lamp off. Madi lay on her soft, pillow.

Madi is still tossing and turning in bed. The caffeine hit her hard. It is close to two o'clock in the morning before she falls asleep, as she can remember seeing her clock. She overslept her usual hour of seven o'clock.

Madi jumps out of bed at ten o'clock. It is Tuesday, today.

Madi is having dinner with her parents, soon.

Madi stops by the store shortly after breakfast. She puts her groceries in the fridge. It is time to get ready for the family dinner.

Madi pulls up to her parent's house at four o'clock. She does not want to be late. Madi wants to spend quality time with the family. They watch her pull into the driveway. Mom, dad, and Brent, all greet her at the front door. Her father just got home from golfing. He is wearing his golf attire. Mom looks like she got in from Sunday church service. Brent is in his every day blue jeans, t-shirt, with a ball cap on backwards. The whole clan. This is they. Brent even dresses as such in the house. Her mother refuses him to wear his sneakers on her clean floors. Welcome to Madi's little family. Madi is five years, Brent's senior. They talk but they have their own lives, peers, and friends. They enjoy their own fun. Brent is the socialite. Madi is reserved and focused. Brent went to church every Sunday. He is the preferred child. Madi does her own thing. Madi prays, reads her Bible, and understands it to be God's word. Madi tries to be content in most everything. God teaches us in his word how we can learn to live in God's abundance.

Madi cannot wait to be back to work. The holiday was great. It is time to go back to work. She enjoys her independence. The choice we face as a Christian is to put our trust in God, every day. God is our provider. He will meet our needs as he promises. When we pray, we need to believe God and trust him to do what he says he will do. He will do as he says when we obey him and trust him at his word.

"Hey, Madi," Brent says. "Come shoot some hoops out back."

"Sure, be right there," Madi says. Madi liked to wrestle with her brother. She mostly liked to drop his ego whenever the chance arose. Oftentimes, she would take it too far, and he ran off in a pout. Brent is a bit of a spoiled mamma's boy. Madi has outgrown this in her life. She lets it alone. It is not her problem, anymore. It is Brent's and her mother's. Madi now enjoys her own peace in her own home.

Madi's mother ran the home. Her father seems a bit of a coward. He works hard, and at the end of the day he wants to put his feet up. Sometimes, he even wants a beer after work. Madi's mother is disgusted to find a pack of six beers in her fridge. Madi can hear her voice now, *"Steven, what is this distasteful stuff in my fridge.*" Madi's father is harmless, he let mom raise us, though. Madi saw her father at dinner time and Sunday church. They went on one family vacation every summer. They did all the right things. Madi home was normal, but no heart for real life.

Madi and Brent sit in their places at the table. Madi's parents sit in theirs. It is like old times. The dinner is ready and set out perfect. Madi's father blesses the food, and they eat their dinner. The table conversation is minimal. They all lead their own lives with not much to say to one another. Madi's mother is lonely. She has no friends. Madi's mother is too involved in other people's lives.

"Thank you for dinner, mother, it is lovely as usual." Madi tries to be polite, but she cannot make her mother happy. It does not matter how hard she tries.

"I do need to head home," Madi replies. "I am a little tired."

"I did not sleep well last night," Madi speaks.

"Thank you for coming, dear," mother says.

"Do not make it so long next time," she says.

"I promise," Madi says. "I have lots happening, this week."

"Thank you," mother says. "I love you very much, Madi."

"I love you, too," Madi says closing the door behind her.

Madi arrives home, closing the front door. She locks it behind her. Madi heads upstairs and crawls into bed with her book beside her. It is a restless night for Madi. Madi is not comfortable in her parents' home. She has her own home, now.

Madi's father is not real. He is passive and not exactly a good example of a church, going father. Madi's mother is the spiritual leader. Madi knows from scripture that her parent's incompatible marriage is the imbalance from her childhood home. The neighbors know it, too. No one says a word, they watch and observe. Madi does hope for good things. She knows in her spirit that her parents' marriage may fail if something does not happen, soon. Her father is unhappy and quiet most days. He works hard to make ends meet. All he did was never enough.

Madi loves her parents, both, and her brother. They are irresponsible. Madi is more distraught most with her father. He is not the man she wants him to be. Madi and Brent were close as young children. Brent learned to manipulate his way to get the things he wanted.

Eight

Madi wakes up at ten o'clock in the morning to the sun shining through her window. It is a beautiful morning. Madi pulls her bed together and jumps into the shower. She dresses and heads down the stairs, by half past ten. She gathers her breakfast fixings: eggs, bread, and butter from the fridge. "Fried eggs and toast and a glass of milk," Madi says to herself.

The telephone rings. She heads over to the table where it lay. It is Ron, her next, door neighbor.

"Hello, Madi," Ron says. "Hope you slept well."

"I did, it was a little restless," Madi replies. "I had dinner with the folks, yesterday."

"Ok, I hope it went well," Ron replies. "Your mother puts on a good spread." The conversation ended there.

"Brenda and I want to ask you to join us for a BBQ, this afternoon," he speaks.

Madi has no plans for the next few days. "I would like that," Madi replies.

Madi enjoys their companionship. They are normal. Their children are on their own. Madi is like one of their own. Ron and Brenda know her well. They are in her life to help her. They are positive role models.

"Come by around four o'clock," Ron says.

"Sounds good," Madi says.

"What can I bring to add to dinner?" Madi asks. "It is right to bring something."

"You do not need to bring anything, this time," Ron replies. "Brenda, has dinner already planned and started."

"You can get the next BBQ date," Ron says.

"Sounds good to me," Madi replies. "I look forward to it." Ron and Madi say goodbye. Madi hangs up the telephone. Madi begins her breakfast preparation. She sits at the table and eats her eggs and toast. Madi tidies the kitchen. She retires to finish her book.

Madi checks the clock. She has time to go for a walk. Madi ties her sneakers and closes the door behind her. Madi sings a favorite song. It is one of those praise songs that fills her spirit with God's joy. Madi can see her reflection in the river. The sun is bright, today. The river is glistening. The geese are home. It amazes Madi. The geese stay around for the winter. She lives near the mountains. The winters can get cold this time of year. The snow fall is plenteous in the mountain village. Madi is a skier. She lives in a ski resort. Liam is a skier, too. It is something they enjoy together.

Madi does not have any reason to go home. She stays late in the park.

Madi arrives at Ron and Brenda's at four o'clock.

Ron and Brenda greet her at the front door with a hug.

"Thank you for coming, today," Brenda says with a smile.

"Thank you for inviting me," Madi replies.

"There are plenty of new things happening," Madi speaks. "I cannot wait to tell you."

"We cannot wait to hear all about your vacation and the new things," Ron replies.

Madi seats herself on the wingback chair in the corner of the front room. "I have a couple of meetings this week," Madi speaks.

"It is all good," Madi says laughing. "I am stepping into new waters and trusting in God, every day."

"You will be fine, Madi," Ron says. "You are strong."

"We will pray for God's wisdom and direction in your life," Ron replies.

"Thank you," Madi says.

"I do not want to say too much," Madi continues. "My parents do not even know, yet."

"It will all work out, Madi, "Ron replies. "God has good things in store for those who love him."

"Thank you," Madi replies.

"You know how difficult my parents are to deal with," Madi continues. "I love them, but I do not want them making my decisions."

"We understand," Brenda says. "Let us eat before it gets cold."

The dinner spread is lovely. Brenda has prepared roast chicken, garlic potatoes, steamed vegetables, and a garden salad.

Ron sets the BBQ chicken on the table.

Madi helps herself to a dinner plate and helps herself to her portion.

"It all looks lovely," Madi says.

"Thank you," Madi speaks. "I am blessed to have you so close to home."

"We are blessed, too," Brenda replies. "You are welcome, anytime."

They eat in quietness. Madi finishes her dinner.

After dinner, Ron cleans the BBQ. Brenda and Madi clear the table. Madi helps Brenda clean the dinner dishes.

Madi is tired. She excuses herself. "Thank you for your hospitality and the fine meal," Madi says. "I am ready to go home."

Ron and Brenda walk Madi to the door. They watch Madi tie her sneakers.

Ron gently takes her arm. "We have your back, Madi," he says. "We are here for you."

"Good night, Madi," Brenda says.

"Good night," Madi replies. Madi closes the door behind her and walks across the street.

Madi unlocks the front door. She locks it behind her. She puts her shoes in the closet. She heads up the stairs and jumps in the shower. She slips into a night gown. Madi grabs her Bible from her bedroom bookshelf. She sits down in her bedroom chair and turns on the lamp. Her Bible opens to Psalm 27. She reads and continues through the Psalms up to and including Psalm 34. And then she prays, asking God to give her the courage to get through the rest of the week.

Madi tucks herself into the comfort of her bed. She is soon asleep.

Nine

Madi wakes to the sound of rain on the windowpanes. It is not unusual to hear it this time of year. She can feel the chill from the floor under her feet. Madi likes the rain. It oftentimes can bring the cold winters around sooner than anticipated. She puts up with it. It goes with the ski hills. Madi is thankful when the sun comes around after a chilly winter day.

Madi looks forward to her new opportunity. She is learning to accept change as a new way of life. The time is ten o'clock. Madi never sleeps this late. She jumps from her bed and pulls the sheets and blankets over the pillows. Madi is hungry. Madi put together a fried egg sandwich on buttered toast with light mayonnaise. She pours herself a glass of milk. She grabs a multi vitamin and sits down to eat.

Madi is chill this morning. After breakfast, she throws her laundry in the washing machine. It is pre-sorted. Madi tidies up her breakfast dishes. She reads three chapters in her new book while she waits for the laundry to finish. She removes the clothes from the washing machine. She hangs her delicate items up to dry. Madi puts the last load into the washing machine.

It is pouring rain outside. She does not feel like walking in this weather. Madi will drive down to the mall, later. She wants to do a little window shopping. Madi is not much of a shopper. There were times she did like to shop. She put the last of the clothes in the dryer.

Madi has her raincoat and sneakers on. She is on her way out the door. Madi cannot wait to get out of the house every day. She jumps in the car. Her seatbelt is fastened. She is off to enjoy a shopping spree. Madi is singing in the car, again. Madi is happy. She likes the changing elements of the air. Madi likes the seasonal changes. Winter is coming, and soon it will be Spring. It is a time of new growth, greenery, baby deer, baby birds and other creatures. Madi arrives at the mall with a glow surrounding her this afternoon. She just knows good things are beginning in her life. She is thankful to God for every blessing in her life.

Madi remembers she needs new shoes for work. There is a Hudson's Bay in the mall near the south end. Madi needs good footwear. She likes to buy the best comfort in a shoe. At the end, of most days, she treated her feet to a good soak. The store clerk can see her looking for a good fit. Madi usually goes with a sketcher. The Hudson Bay does not carry them. Madi shares her thoughts with the clerk. He brings her a couple of options in her size. "You are a size seven, is that correct?" he asks.

Madi is impressed. "Yes," she replies. He finds two pairs. One is a slip on, and the other is a tie on, they both have enough support. Madi walks the aisle with each pair. Madi chooses the tie on. It seems more practical. She does not want her shoes slipping off during her workday.

"Thank you for your help, Brian," Madi says. She takes the box of shoes from the clerk. Madi walks to the till. She pays for the purchase. Madi passes by all the clothing shops. She does not need any new clothes. Madi passes by the Source. She does not need any electronics. She keeps that to a minimum. Her telephone, laptop, TV, and radio are more than enough. Madi does not even watch TV, nor does she listen much to the radio. Madi checks her emails once a day. The telephone is her main point of contact. She likes her life. Madi works hard to maintain it.

Madi missed her normal lunch hour. Her stomach is saying so. She stops at the Subway and orders her turkey breast and cheddar sandwich. One of her favorite meals out.

It is near five-thirty when Madi arrives home. She parks the car and locks the door. Madi opens the front door and closes it quietly behind her. She hangs up her coat and puts her shoes away in the closet. The rain has stopped to a slight, pitter, patter on the roof. It is running down the outside of her windows.

Madi scurries around the kitchen. She is looking for something simple to prepare for dinner. She makes a chicken sandwich. Madi grabs a glass of water and retires to the front room. She sits in her favorite front room chair. She turns on the TV and surfs the channels for something to view. There are a couple of movies later she might enjoy. She finds an old drama to amuse herself over dinner and the next hour. Madi turns the TV off. Madi's lights are going out at ten o'clock, tonight.

Madi walks upstairs to her bedroom. Tomorrow is Friday, it will be a big day. Next is her date night on Saturday. Madi undresses and pulls her night gown over her head. She does a quick brush of her teeth. She is ready for bed. It has been another full day. She crawls between the clean sheets and lays on her pillow. She steps out of bed to draw the curtains to darken the room. Madi crawls back into bed.

Madi falls asleep.

Ten

"Ugh, another rainy day," Madi thinks aloud. It chills her bones. It will turn to snow, soon. Skiing season will arrive. Madi is certain she and Liam will discuss their first skiing trip of the season, on Saturday night. They have done it for years. Madi does not want to get out of bed this morning. It is only ten o'clock. She slept in again.

Madi will soon be back to work. She enjoys getting up for work every day. She enjoys earning her own living. Madi is looking forward to new things.

Madi gets out of bed. She looks for a comfortable sweater in her closet. Madi's closet is tidy. She is careful with her laundry. She believes in maintaining her clothes. It keeps them longer. She lays her clothes on her bed and makes her way to the shower. She likes the feeling of the warm water and the suds falling around her shoulders and her body. She dries her body and wraps the towel around her head. Madi dresses.

Madi runs her fingers through her hair and lets it hang down. She touches her eyes with a light mascara and a little eye shadow. It is just enough for a little enhancement. It will soon be lunchtime.

Madi looks through her pantry. She finds a tin of mushroom soup. She puts it in a pot to heat. She has time to relax before her meeting at three o'clock. She is only twenty minutes from the diner. She finishes her lunch. It leads her to a new perspective for the day.

It is still raining. She will skip the walk today. It is time to find a new book. Madi finds her way to her bookshelf in the front room. Madi is a collector of classic novels. She has a copy of *Pilgrim's Progress, A Girl of the Limberlost*, these are not her favorite. She has inherited them from her mother's bookshelf of duplicates. She has her worn Bible from her teen years. Madi has a new reference Bible that she purchased for her own studying. She collects various books to study other religions. She believes it is good to understand those of other faiths. She pulls out her copy of *Heidi*. It is an oldie and a fun read.

Madi reads until the time is near to meet with Liam and Doris.

The clock reads two o'clock. It is time to head to the diner. She does not want to be late. Madi arrives at two twenty-five.

"Hello, Madi," Liam says. "I am happy to see you, this afternoon."

"Grab a cup of coffee and a donut. Liam replies. "We will sit down, soon."

"You read my thoughts, Liam," Madi replies.

"Thank you." Liam turns to look at Madi and smiles.

Madi pours herself a coffee and adds a couple of creamers. Her eyes search the pastry plate. She reaches for a chocolate glazed donut. She seats herself at the staff table. Madi reads the newspaper. The local news is always the same. Madi sips her coffee and slowly eats her donut. Madi is lost in thought when Liam arrives. He sits in the chair across from her.

"Madi," Liam says. "I think the three of us will meet in my office."

"I will be ready in five minutes," he replies.

"Doris is finishing up with something," Liam says. "She will join us, soon."

"Ok, I will meet you there," Madi smiles. Liam stands up and heads to his office. Madi finishes her coffee and the last bite of her donut. She grabs her dishes and drops them in the wash basin.

Madi heads toward Liam's office.

Madi knocks on his door.

"Come in and have a seat," Liam answers.

Madi sits quietly in the far chair across from Liam.

Liam can see Doris walking over to the office. He smiles to welcome her.

"Hello, Madi," Doris says. "Welcome back, it is so nice to see you, today."

"Madi, we have made some changes around here," Liam speaks, next.

"The main one is ownership," Liam continues. "I have asked Doris to come on as a partner in the business."

"We are looking at expansion options," he explains. "We need your help to fill in the gaps in the lack."

"We are asking you to remain on staff with your old duties," Liam says, "with an extension of duties."

"Some of these duties will include assisting management with the day-to-day operations," he continues." "It will come with a raise."

"Doris and I have put together an agreement in the form of an offer." Liam says handing a sealed envelope across the desk to Madi.

"Take it home and read it," Liam says. "If you agree, please resume your duties on Monday."

Madi reaches for the envelope and smiles at Liam and then at Doris.

"Thank you," Madi replies. "I will review it, carefully."

"Will I see you tomorrow evening? Madi asks Liam.

"Yes," Liam replies. "I will pick you up at six o'clock at your door."

Madi says good-bye to both Liam and Doris. She thanks them for their time and heads toward the door. Madi is smiling. She is excited for new things. Madi drives home in quietness. The radio is off. She whispers a prayer of thanksgiving to God.

Madi pulls into her driveway. She steps into the house. She quietly closes the front door behind her. She hangs up her coat and puts her shoes away in the closet.

Madi plugs in the kettle to make a cup of tea. She prepares her tea and sits at the kitchen table.

Madi opens the brown, sealed envelope. It is a one-page document.

"Yes, that is just like Liam," she says to herself.

Madi likes Liam's style. Liam is a performer and lover at heart, without all the extra complications.

Liam likes things simple. He clearly states her duties and the terms of payment in the document.

Madi is happy. She signs and dates the contract.

Madi dials Liam's telephone number.

"Hello, Madi," Liam answers.

"Thank you," Madi says. "I accept."

"Thank you," Liam says. "I cannot wait to see you tomorrow evening, no business talk."

"It is a deal," Madi replies.

"Get some rest," Liam replies. "I am still the boss!" "I have some paperwork to finish."

"Good night, Madi."

"Good night, Liam."

It is cool in the evenings now. Madi wraps up in a warm coat and heads out for a walk. She needs fresh air. She will come back in later for a quick bite to eat, and an early night.

Saturday will come, soon. If she knows Liam, he will make an entrance. She loves him.

Liam is a businessperson with a friendly character.

Eleven

Madi wakes early, Saturday morning. She moves around the house doing her usual Saturday morning chores. She decides what to wear for the evening out. She likes her red sweater. It will look great with her grey dress pants. She will wear her black dress pumps. She seldom wears heels. This evening she just wants to feel pretty. Well, that settles things. She puts her crazy, girl thoughts away for the moment. Madi still has time left in her day.

The sun is bright. After breakfast, Madi goes for a walk around the neighborhood. She will stop by Ron and Brenda's for tea. Madi puts her dishes in the kitchen sink. She does not normally do this. She wants to enjoy the sunshine and blue sky before the snow falls. She slips her shoes on and throws her coat over her shoulders. She puts her arms in the sleeves on the way out the door. She locks the door behind her.

Madi skips down the sidewalk. She is singing a gentle song. She is happy, today. All things have worked out as she has prayed.

Madi must remember to call her parents.

Madi steps up to Ron and Brenda's sidewalk. They are outside preparing their yard before the snow falls.

"Hello, Madi," Ron says. Brenda is smiling behind him.

"You look happy," Ron speaks. "Keep singing, girl."

"Have you talked to your parents, yet?" Brenda asks.

"Not yet," Madi replies.

"I will tomorrow night," Madi says. "I hope they will be happy for me."

"They will, Madi, be patient," Brenda replies. "It is hard to let your children grow up."

"I will stop by tomorrow, afternoon," Madi says. "I should tell my parents first."

"That is a good idea," Ron replies.

"Thank you," Madi says.

"We love you, Madi," Brenda replies. "See you tomorrow."

Madi says goodbye. She is looking forward to the evening with Liam. She has no expectations.

Madi wants to be at her best.

Madi crosses the road and walks up her driveway. She closes the front door behind her. She hangs up her coat. She puts away her shoes in the closet. Madi remembers her dishes in the sink. She heads upstairs to her bedroom for a nap. She is looking forward to her evening out. Madi makes herself comfortable. She pulls the blanket around her and falls asleep.

Madi fell asleep for two hours. She stands up and goes downstairs to wash her breakfast dishes. She cuts up an apple and enjoys a handful of carrots. It will hold her until dinner. Madi heads back upstairs to freshen up. She jumps into a warm shower. She slips into her slacks and sweater. She puts on a touch of light makeup. She carries her black pumps to the front door.

Madi has a beautiful khaki, knee length over coat she likes to wear when she dresses up. Mostly, it is for church and evenings out. Madi cannot remember the last time she wore it. She feels like a respectable lady. It is a beautiful feeling. Madi is done with the fancy stuff for, now. She is ready. It is four-thirty.

Liam will arrive at six o'clock.

Madi surfs her TV to pass the time.

Liam arrives. It is five minutes to six when she hears his truck pull up in the driveway. Liam sits in the truck for ten minutes. He is nervous, today. Tonight, is different. Liam has stepped up to the plate. He knows he wants to marry, Madi. He wants to make her happy and see her dreams happen. Liam hopes and prays he can make her happy. She is already an important integral, part of his life. It makes sense.

"God give me the courage to lead the life I have chosen," Liam prays.

"Give us the courage to walk together, Amen." Liam is at peace. He opens the truck door and steps onto the driveway. He closes the truck door behind him. He walks up to the front door and knocks twice.

Madi is waiting at the door. She smiles as he walks inside the house.

"Hello, Madi," Liam says. They are both nervous. They have stepped into new waters. They are out of their comfort zone. They are both timid. They have enjoyed a beautiful, long-term friendship.

Madi is going to have to rely on her faith in God and pray through her fears.

"Are we ready to go?" Liam asks breaking the silence. "I am hungry."

"Yes," she smiles up at him.

Liam stands six feet, two inches beside Madi's five feet four inches. They look great together. Liam puts his arm around her touching the small part of her back. He opens the truck door. He gives Madi a hand into the truck. He gets in beside her. They buckle up, and Liam puts the truck in gear. They are off to find a nice place for dinner.

"I did not make reservations," Liam says. "I thought we could decide on the road trip." It is Liam's kind of adventure. Liam knows what she likes. They work together. He feeds her most days.

"I feel like a burger and a shake," Madi says with a smile.

"I can go for that, too," Liam replies.

"Have you ever been to Smiley's on the other end of town?" he asks.

"No," Madi nods her head.

"I think you will like it," Liam says. "It is a simple, diner." Liam turns the truck around at the next stop. He misses the turn while they are talking.

Madi watches him drive. She sits quietly in the truck awaiting the next stop.

"We will be there in five minutes, Madi," Liam says.

"Sounds good, Liam," Madi replies. "I am hungry." She grabs her purse and sits it on her lap.

Liam pulls into the parking lot. He shuts the truck off and steps outside. He walks around to help Madi out of the truck. She likes the way that Liam treats her.

"Thank you," Madi replies. Madi and Liam walk inside together.

Liam holds the door for Madi. He follows close behind her.

Madi and Liam wait for a server to find a seat.

It is not too long before a server walks towards them. He offers them a quiet seat for two. They accept a corner seat near the fireplace.

Madi likes the warmth.

Liam likes it when Madi is comfortable. She removes her outside jacket, and Liam does the same. There is a coat rack next to their table where they hang their coats.

Liam sits across the table from Madi. He smiles at her.

"You have beautiful eyes, Madi," he says.

"Thank you," Madi replies. She felt her cheeks blush. She is not good with compliments about herself.

The server pours two glasses of water.

Madi and Liam each order a mushroom, cheddar burger. a caesar side salad with a medium milkshake.

Madi orders strawberry, and Liam a vanilla. It is a beautiful moment between friends.

Madi breaks the silence. "We have not been out together like this for a long time," she smiles.

"I apologize," Liam replies. "I have been caught up with life and overlooked our friendship."

"Madi, I do not want to lose you," Liam says. "You are my best friend."

Madi feels the same, but she is not always so outspoken.

"I care about you very much, Madi," Liam says. "I want more for us."

"I am thankful for Ron and Brenda in your life," Liam continues.

"You manage your life well and still keep a positive composure," Liam says. "You are a beautiful, Christian woman."

"Thank you, Liam," Madi replies. Those are the kindest words she has ever heard.

Madi keeps her distance from most people, but Liam is different.

"Madi, I owe you an apology," Liam says.

"I know I was abrupt about my faith," he speaks. "I was hard on you."

"My grandmother was a Christian," Liam says. "I loved her the most."

"She married a man because she was pregnant with my father out of wedlock," he continues. "He lived unhappy in the middle of a battleground."

"They were hardworking people," Liam continues. "My father's unhappy childhood caused him to leave the church." "My grandmother taught us as best she could in the way of her faith."

"Madi, I gave my life to the Lord as a child," Liam says. "I never forgot that day."

"I know the Lord came into my life," Liam replies. "I felt different, but I never really did get into the Bible."

"I cannot believe you are telling me this, tonight," Madi replies. "You kept this to yourself all of these years."

"I was not ready to share it until now," Liam continues. "I realize, now, we have so much to give to each other." "I believe God brought me to this place in my life, Madi."

The food arrives. The server sets the plates down on the table. Madi cuts her burger in half, and Liam the same. It is good diner etiquette. Madi takes a bite and sets her burger back on the plate.

"Thank you for telling me," Madi replies.

"I have read my Bible," Madi continues. "Maybe we can study, together."

"I would love to share my learned knowledge with you," Madi says. "I believe God speaks to me when I read his word." Madi's quiet spirit smiles back at Liam.

Liam smiles and eats his burger.

"Good choice," Madi says changing the topic.

"Yes," Liam says.

"Am I going to have to say it often?" Liam laughs looking across at Madi.

Madi smiles, "most likely." "How about I be right half the time and you the other half."

Now Liam laughs, again. "If only it were that easy." They finish their dinner settling into friendly conversation sipping milkshakes. It is Saturday night and nearing nine o'clock.

Madi and Liam have both had a long day.

"I am sorry there has been so much excitement in the last couple of days," Madi replies. "I am almost ready for bed."

"I understand," Liam replies. Liam grabs their jackets and helps Madi into hers.

The server can see they are getting ready to leave. He walks over to the table and accepts Liam's payment.

Thank you for the dinner," Liam says to the server.

Madi nods her approval and smiles at the server.

Liam guides her to the front door. Madi does not resist Liam's help. He helps her up into the truck.

Liam starts the truck, and they are off to Madi's home.

Liam arrives at Madi's a brief time later. He walks her to the front door and waits while she unlocks the door.

Madi smiles and thanks him for the wonderful evening. She wants to ask him something but stops.

"Good night, Madi," Liam says. Liam put his arms around her and hugged her, he gently offers her a kiss on her left cheek.

"Good night, Liam," she replies closing the door behind her. Madi is ready for bed. She removes her shoes and drops her jacket on the hall chair on the way by. She heads straight upstairs to her little bedroom. She dresses in a clean night gown and crawls into bed. She almost forgot to say a prayer. She rests for a bit and falls asleep.

Madi wakes up to a bright, Sunday morning. It is Madi's day off this week.

Monday will be business, as usual.

On this Sunday Madi gets up, eats her breakfast, and sets out to enjoy a long walk.

Madi sits in her chair with a good book and her Bible by her side.

Twelve

Madi hears the alarm go off at six o'clock in the morning. It startles her. It is still time to sleep. Madi has a smile on her face. It feels good to be going back to work. She likes her regular routine. It is going to be different at the diner for all of them. She will manage one day at a time. Her extra duties will bring challenges. Now, the business of dating the boss, too. She will have to learn to deal with it. There will be more work and more responsibility. She now has personal obligations to the diner.

Madi smiles. She is thankful for all the good things in her life.

Madi arrives at ten o'clock. She is anxious to orientate herself back to the old routine. She wants a good cup of coffee and the local news to read. She cannot wait to see her regular customers.

Madi meets Liam at the front entrance. "Good morning, Madi," Liam says smiling.

"Good morning, Liam," Madi replies.

"I would like a coffee," she says. "It is good be back."

"Help yourself," he replies. "It is ready." "It is good to have you back."

"In the next few weeks," Liam says. "You will move forward with your regular duties."

"Regarding our lives personal is personal," Liam says with a smile, "and business is business."

Madi smiles assuredly pouring herself a cup of coffee. She grabs a seat and sips her coffee quietly in the corner. She browses the newspaper. It is always the same advertisements and the blah, blah news. Madi keeps herself free of the profanity and the negative. It disgusts her.

It is time for Madi to work. Doris is ready. Madi lays out the salad bar fixings, fills the cutlery, refreshes the condiments and the coffee bar.

Madi finishes her tasks. The customers begin to arrive. Madi washes her hands and hurries to greet them. Madi smiles at the young couple. They indicate they would like a quiet table to be alone.

Madi directs them to a two-seat table away from the window. She offers them a coffee and a water. She leaves the lunch menus on the table. "I will be back soon," Madi says.

"Thank you," the gentleman replies. "Give us fifteen minutes." Madi nods and smiles.

Madi seats her next customer and then the next as they arrive, one at a time.

Liam steps in when her hands are full. The diner has a full-service plan that consists of six tables per server.

Madi tends to her tables offering beverages and lunch menus. She gives her customers space to make their choices. Madi remains attentive throughout her shift to their needs. She maintains beverages and serves hot food as it comes ready. Madi cleans the tables as they become available. She is careful to set them up promptly. Liam relies on her efficiency and her customers, too. She has many regulars.

Madi has a full day, today. She will work both lunch and dinner hours right through the day. There are days she will do a split shift and go home for a couple of hours. Her feet would be tired. It is all good. She knows she will recover. She always does. Madi paces herself through her day. After Christmas, they will get back to their regular shifts when business slows down.

Liam promises he will find a part time server to fill in a couple of days per week. He wants his staff to have a life outside of work. He, too, believes in work and life balance.

Madi looks forward to this. He promises they will share a day together, soon. It will be a good time to catch up. They have so much to share with each other. Madi is patient with Liam. She knows good things are in store for her life.

Madi has yet to share any of her news with her parents. The right time will come. It will happen. She wants Liam to be a part of the moment. A nice quiet dinner party will be nice.

Liam decides it is best to wait. He wants to prove himself. Liam loves Madi and he wants her confident.

Madi and Liam pray God will take their relationship in a new direction for him. Madi asks God to show her every day. The dinner hour is approaching. Madi has all the preparations complete. The customers start arriving. One by one she serves each one of them.

The end of the evening arrives. Madi helps Doris finalize the last dishes. Madi grabs her coat. She says good-bye and heads home.

Madi arrives to the quietness of her beautiful home. She settles in a hot soaking bath for her aching feet. She ate at the diner. She is not hungry.

Madi prepares herself for bed. Her alarm is set. She crawls under the sheets.

Madi falls asleep.

Tuesday morning brings the usual routine into Madi's life. Wednesday and Thursday are the same as usual.

Liam offers her Friday off.

Madi gratefully accepts. She will tidy the house, Thursday evening, and do her laundry. It will give Madi time to go for a drive on Friday. She will spend some time alone.

The next day came early. Liam is not at the diner when she arrives. It is very unusual. Doris advises Madi he will be running late. Something came up today that he needs to manage. She indicates he will be in later this afternoon.

Liam usually keeps her informed. Madi finds it strange. She shrugs it off and goes back to work. It is none of her business.

Tuesday comes to the end of the shift and no Liam. She grabs her jacket and heads out of the door. It is a quiet drive home. Madi is not in the mood for any background noise. She is concerned about Liam. He did not call her.

Madi arrives home. Tonight, will be a quick shower to wipe off the dirt of the day. Madi is in the dark of her front room. She turns on the lamp beside her chair. Her Bible is on the table. She opens it and reads a scripture passage. She loves re-reading the books of the New Testament. Madi lays down the Bible.

Madi reaches for her telephone. It is nine-fifteen. Madi contemplates. She knows he will be up. She dials Liam's number.

Liam answers the telephone on the second ring.

"Hello," Liam answers.

"Good evening, Liam," Madi says. "I missed you, today."

"I missed you, too," Liam replies.

"Is everything ok?" Madi asks.

"I fell ill, last night," Liam says. "I went in to see the doctor today after the bank meeting."

"I will be fine in a few days," Liam replies. "I need rest."

"Don't worry it will all be good, soon," he says.

"Will you be in tomorrow?" Madi asks.

"Probably not," Liam replies, "the doctor suggests I take some days off to rest."

"Can you manage things?" he asks.

"Of course, I can," Madi replies. "I will work Friday."

"I will let you know if I need you," Liam replies.

"Thank you," Liam says. "Good night, hon, I love you."

"I love you too," Madi whispers. "Good night!" Madi turns out the lamp.

Madi crawls into bed.

Madi needs sleep. She says a prayer for Liam's recovery.

Madi falls asleep.

The week goes by and still no Liam, at the diner. Madi continues in prayer for him each night before bed.

Doris asks her Thursday morning to cover Friday's shift.

Madi agrees.

Doris smiles and thanks her.

"How is Liam doing?" Madi asks.

"He is recovering," Doris replies. "He wants to be back to work on Monday."

"If you can work through Sunday, please take Monday and Tuesday off," Doris says. "I would appreciate it."

"We will get back to normal as soon as possible," Doris speaks. "He has been working hard."

"He wants to take more scheduled time off," Doris continues. "We will hire another full-time staff soon."

"Thank you for letting me know," Madi replies. "Good night, Doris."

"Good night, Madi," Doris replies.

Madi worries. She knows she needs to be strong. Madi continues to pray for Liam, and the workload at the diner.

Madi does not call Liam, tonight. He needs his rest. She does want to be with him.

Thirteen

Friday morning came, too, early. Madi is covering at the diner today and on the weekend for Liam. Madi prays he will recover for Monday. She needs time to herself, too. Madi's feet ache. She jumps out of bed. She does not want to be late nor let Liam down. Liam is depending on her.

Madi scurries around her typical morning duties. She wants to get to the diner each morning by ten o'clock to enjoy a coffee and a couple slices of toast before her morning duties. She needs to help Doris with the extra duties at the diner. Liam will have so much extra paperwork to do.

Madi speeds to the diner. She arrives a bit before ten o'clock. She parks her car and locks the doors. She puts her keys in her pocket. Madi walks up to the front door. She is startled by a voice behind her.

"Good morning, Madi," Liam says.

Madi turns around to see him. She smiles up at Liam. He looks pale and tired.

"How are you feeling?" Madi asks.

"I am eighty/twenty," Liam replies comfortably.

"I need to get some things caught up," Liam continues. "The work does not stop."

"I have been doing too much and not eating properly," Liam replies. "I need to make a few lifestyle changes, the doctor says."

Madi looks at him again. "You look pale."

"I am a little low on iron," Liam says. "It takes time to heal."

"The doctor says a few weeks of rest and meal replacement will do me good," Liam speaks. "I am going to rely on you more."

"We need a couple more staff," Liam replies. "I want you to help me more."

"I will close the diner for a couple of days if I need to." Liam speaks. "You and Doris need your rest, too."

"I hope it will not come to that," Madi speaks.

"We can talk more, later," Liam says. "I need to get some work done."

"Stop by the house this weekend and we can talk," Liam says.

Madi is glad for the offer. She indicates she would stop by, Saturday evening, after work.

Madi enjoys a quick coffee and a banana for breakfast. It will suffice until her lunch period between shifts, today. Madi needs to eat proper to keep strong. She works hard.

Friday is busy. It is not long before Madi will be heading home.

Her Friday night is blissful. Madi retires to enjoy a hot soaking bath. She heads to bed early.

Saturday comes early. The bright sun shining in her window. Madi arrives at work. She sits down with her cup of coffee and her usual breakfast.

Saturdays can be fun. Madi is always on the go. It is usually full of locals that like to hang out. Liam must put a limit on their stay. He tries to be fair as best he can. They are understanding. He often must remind the guests the diner is a business place.

The day goes by quickly. Soon, Madi is heading out the front door to her car. She arrives at her door at seven-fifteen. She jumps in the shower and puts on a clean pair of slacks and a light sweater. Madi will be heading over to Liam's house.

Madi gives Liam a quick call to let him know she is on her way.

Madi speeds towards Liam's house. She arrives at seven forty-five. It will be a short visit. She wants to catch up and check in on him.

Madi knocks on the door and Liam opens it. He is waiting for her.

"Hello Madi," Liam says hugging her. Liam thanks her for coming over.

"Hello Liam," Madi says with a warm smile.

Liam offers her a seat in the front room. He plugs in the kettle for a cup of tea.

"We need to catch up," Madi says.

"How are you feeling?" Madi asks.

"I am feeling better," Liam replies. "The doctor says so, too."

"He says I need to slow down the pace," he replies.

"It is easy to say," Liam says. "The diner is busy."

"I am running a business and the margins have only so much room," Liam continues.

"Good people are hard to find like you," Liam replies. "We need to hire at least one more body."

"I want to balance our working hours," he continues further. "I do not want to burn Doris out, nor you."

Madi nods her head, affirmative.

"I am going to rely on you more," Liam replies. "I will insist you take your time away from the diner."

"I still want you to pursue an education at some point," Liam says.

Madi looks at him. She does not have any interest in college. She is not ready for the commitment.

"I will sit down with you on Monday," Liam says. "I am feeling better, every day."

"I want you to get involved in the office," Liam continues. "It will give me a day off and peace of mind."

Madi is eager to learn and grow in the business. She looks forward to learning new things.

"I would like to help you," Madi replies. "It is good to learn new things."

"Enough shop talk," Liam speaks.

"How are you doing, Madi?" Liam asks.

"I am good," Madi says. "I am tired at the end of the day."

"It is all good," Madi replies. "I know this pace is temporary."

"Are you still comfortable with the dating scene?" Liam asks.

"Of course," Madi says. "I am not a quitter."

"I do not expect, too, much," Madi replies.

"I look forward to spending time together, again," Madi continues. "I follow my life where it leads."

"I am not ready to get married, tomorrow," Madi says. "I am going to let life happen in its own time."

"I appreciate your maturity, Madi," Liam says.

"Thank you," Madi replies.

"I am behind you, Madi," Liam replies.

"You are a strong person," Liam says. "You are the one I want to spend the rest of my life with." "I need you in my life."

"I need you, too," Madi replies.

"It is getting late," Madi says. "I should be getting home."

"Thank you for stopping by," Liam says.

"I love you," Liam whispers.

"I love you, too," Madi replies. Madi steps out the front door and into her car. She drives home quietly. Madi yawns. She arrives home and locks the front door and heads up to bed.

Madi lay in bed. One more day this week to get through. Sundays are busy days.

Madi falls asleep in the comfort of her bed.

Fourteen

Madi wakes up early, Sunday morning. She jumps in the shower, ties her hair back and brushes her teeth. Madi has little extra time these days. She sits in her chair and grabs her Bible. It seems so long since Madi has had time to read. Madi pours over the psalms. Madi loves to pray and sing the words of David's prayers when life gets tough.

Madi sips her coffee at the diner, this morning, nibbling on a piece of toast. She is not so eager to be on her feet this morning. The breakfast customers are beginning to arrive. They are early, again. The diner does not open until nine o'clock on Sunday. Madi pulls herself together. She puts her best smile on her face and steps into her regular tasks.

Madi says a prayer to the Lord to get her through her day. Her heart fills with joy. She unlocks the front door. Her heart is full of love but her feet ache. Madi will persevere, again.

Madi did it. Another day is done. She closes the door behind her. She jumps in her car and heads home.

Later at home, Madi finds her bed neatly made and falls asleep on the warm comforter.

Madi wakes a couple of times through the night. The second time she hears the telephone ringing. Madi pulls herself up to reach for the telephone. It stops ringing. It is dark and she can barely read the numbers. She can read enough to know it is Liam's number. She dials back his number on the telephone. It is eight-thirty in the evening.

"Hello," Liam says.

"Hello," Madi replies.

"I am sorry to wake you, Madi," Liam replies. "You must be exhausted."

"I want you to take Monday and Tuesday off, this week," Liam continues. "I have put an advertisement in the newspaper for a new hire."

"I will have a fixed schedule for all of us, soon," Liam says.

"Sounds good," Madi replies. "I am not going to argue."

"Thank you," Liam says, "Good night!"

"Good night," Madi replies hanging up the telephone. Madi is relieved. She lay down on her pillow and falls asleep.

Madi wakes at midnight. She is hungry. "*It is too late to eat*," she thinks to herself. Madi cuts up an apple. She enjoys a small glass of milk.

Soon, Madi is asleep.

Fifteen

Madi wakes to the rain pouring down on the windowpane. It is cold outside. The winter season is approaching. It is a lovely thought. Madi and Liam will hit the ski hills. It is difficult to get away from work, but they will manage a trip or two. Madi hopes. They may have to go alone a time or two.

The thought brings serenity to Madi's mind. She loves the fresh smell of the winter air. She loves the way the pure snow lay as a clean blanket over the dusty, trodden earth. It is a season of cleansing for the earth. The ski hill is a time for Madi to have her fun. It is nearing ten-thirty. It is time for Madi to get herself out of her bed and into a warm shower. She slips into comfortable slacks and a warm sweater. Madi adjusts the thermometer in the room enough to remove the chill in the air.

Madi has her coffee pot brewing. She puts a couple of slices of toast in the toaster. She makes a quick adjustment to the toaster. The toaster has been making dark toast lately. Madi grabs the milk from the fridge and the toast pops up. She butters her toast and adds a small amount of raspberry jam to her liking. She pours herself a cup of coffee setting it on her breakfast table.

Madi asks God to bless her food and to give her a good day.

Madi is enjoying the morning to herself. It has been a long week. She is going to let her mind and body relax, today. She picks up her dishes and lays them in the sink. Madi fills her coffee cup and heads to the front room. She sits in her favorite chair. She turns the TV on hoping to find something interesting to watch. She laughs to herself, "*not at this time of the day.*" She ran threw her personal movie collection.

Madi has watched them all. She declines and plays music softly in the background. She sips her coffee and reads her book. Madi whispers a quiet prayer of gratitude to her faithful God for a home and provisions.

Madi hears the telephone ring. She ignores it.

Madi stands up and takes her coffee cup to the sink. She grabs her telephone on the way back to her chair. Madi sees her mother has called. Madi makes herself comfortable for the telephone call.

"Hello," mother answers.

"Hello," Madi replies.

"I am not ignoring you," Madi says. "I have been very busy."

"We have not heard from you in a while." mother says.

Madi gives little information. "There is lots going on at work," she says.

"I am glad you are busy," mother replies. "I hope he is paying you well."

"I cannot complain." Madi says. "I love my work." Madi can feel the reservations from the other side of the telephone. It makes her feel uncomfortable. "They are good people."

"I will come for dinner when I see my new schedule," Madi says.

"Maybe I can bring a friend?" Madi asks. She waits for affirmation.

"We can discuss it later," mother says.

"Say hello to Brent for me," Madi says. "How is he doing?"

"He is fine," mother replies. "I am glad you are fine."

"Goodbye," mother says.

"Goodbye," Madi says.

Madi is back in her quiet moment when the telephone rings. This time it is Liam.

"Good morning, Liam," Madi says.

"Good morning, beautiful," Liam replies.

"The lunch rush is done," Liam says. "I have a few minutes to talk."

"I am good, enjoying some quiet time," Madi says. "I spoke with my mother."

"I did want to set up a dinner date for us all," Madi says.

"I did not get the response that I was hoping for," Madi replies.

"Do not worry about it, Madi," Liam says. "It will happen in the right time."

"I love you," Liam says.

"You are not a slave to this place," Liam replies. "I want a future together."

"Thank you," Madi says.

"I do want to go to school," she says. "I am not ready, yet."

"Enjoy your days off," Liam replies. "You can call in the evenings to talk."

"Thank you, Liam," Madi replies. "I love you, too."

Sixteen

Madi has time to enjoy her Monday afternoon. It is cold outside, today. She wants to get outside for some fresh air. A walk will do her good. She puts her over boots on top of her sneakers. She buttons her jacket and closes the door behind her. Ron waves to her from the front of his house. Ron and Brenda are shuffling stuff around in the garage, doing winter clean up. Madi walks across the street to meet them.

"Hello," Ron says with Brenda smiling up at her.

"We have not seen much of you around, lately," Ron speaks. "The diner must be keeping you busy."

"I suppose so," she smiles back.

"I do not want to say, too, much," Madi says. "It is Liam's business."

"Would you like to have a hot cocoa with us soon?" Brenda asks.

"I would like a hot cocoa," Madi replies.

Ron and Brenda tidy up a little around the garage and head inside.

Madi follows.

Brenda plugs the kettle in.

Madi puts her footwear on the boot shelf and lays her coat on the chair. She follows Brenda into the kitchen. She sits herself comfortably at the dining room table. Madi is always welcome in their home. She can see her own front door from the bay window of their home.

Ron follows next through the door.

Brenda prepares three cups of cocoa. She slices banana bread for each of them.

"Thank you for the invite," Madi says. "It has been a couple of long weeks."

"This is my first day off in a week and a half," Madi speaks. "Liam took some time off."

"Is he Ok," Ron replies.

"I think so, he needs rest," Madi says, "He has been working too hard."

"I am hoping to find balance, again, soon," she replies.

"I want my home life back," Madi says.

"You need that, Madi," Ron says. "It is a reward of working hard."

"Enjoy your cocoa," Brenda says.

"I will, Brenda, thank you," Madi says taking her first sip of cocoa. Madi enjoys the hot beverage. She helps herself to a piece of banana bread.

Ron and Brenda look at her face. They can see something is different about Madi.

They smile at her.

"Is life treating you well?" Brenda asks.

"I cannot complain," Madi says. "I am working long days, again."

"Liam and I are close again the way we used to be," Madi looks like she wants to say more.

"I see," Ron says.

"It is nice he is stepping up to the plate," Brenda replies. "We are happy for you both."

"I think I am going to head home," Madi says. "I feel like a hot soaking bath and bed."

"May I bring dinner over around six-thirty?" Brenda asks.

Madi smiles and accepts. She has nothing prepared.

"I need to get a few breakfast and weekend groceries," Madi replies. "I eat mainly at the diner."

"Thank you, for your hospitality," Madi says.

Madi walks to the entry way. She puts her shoes on with her jacket over her shoulders. She pulls her arms through the sleeves.

Ron opens the doors for Madi.

She fastens the door behind her. Madi walks home. She heads upstairs to prepare her warm bath.

Madi lay in the bath. Her feet are wrinkled and soft. It is time to get out. She dries herself and gets into her warm pajamas. She walks down the steps and unfastens her front door.

Ron and Brenda will be over with dinner, soon.

The doorbell rings on time. Ron and Brenda arrive. Brenda hands her the plate.

"Mmm," Madi says.

Madi greets them at the front door.

"Thank you," Madi says with a smile. "I appreciate it so much."

Madi offers them a seat.

Ron looks at Brenda, and Brenda back at Ron, with a nod. They remove their shoes and follow Madi to the kitchen.

"Would you like a cup of tea?" Madi asks plugging in the kettle.

Madi set three mugs on the table. They both smile and nod. She covers the plate and puts it in the microwave. She removes the plate and sets it to cool. Madi prepares the pot of tea for her friends. Madi grabs her plate with the potholders setting it on the placemat.

Madi sets out a plate of lemon cookies. She does not want to eat in front of them.

Madi sits down.

Madi can smell the aroma of sauce and pasta. She is hungry. Madi leaves nothing on her plate.

"It is really great," Madi says. "I am forever grateful."

"It is not very often that I get a home cooked meal," Madi says. "I try on the weekends but some days I am too, tired." Madi empties her plate and rinses it in the sink. She places it in the dishwasher.

Ron finishes his tea and stands up from the table, first. "We should be going home," Ron says.

"The ball game is on tonight at eight o'clock."

"I want to be in bed, early," Ron says.

Brenda nods.

"Me, too," Madi replies. "The lights will be out by nine o'clock, here." Madi walks them to the door.

"Good night," she says giving them each a hug.

"Good night," Brenda replies.

"Good night, kid," Ron says.

Madi smiles as they walk back towards their home. She watches them walk the short distance. She fastens the door behind her and locks it. It is eight o'clock. Madi undresses quietly in her bedroom. She slips on her warm pajamas.

Madi eyes are tired. The lights are out in the house. She tucks herself into her bed.

Madi is soon, asleep.

Seventeen

Madi wakes up later than usual on Tuesday morning. It is her day off.

She puts together her favorite breakfast and sips her morning coffee. She has no idea what to do with her day. The winter months are settling in. There is little snow on the ground. You could feel it in the air. She finishes her breakfast and lays the dishes in the sink.

Madi reaches for the telephone and makes herself comfortable in her chair.

She dials Liam at the diner.

Liam answers.

"Hello, Liam, how are you feeling?" Madi asks.

"I am doing better, and you?" Liam asks.

"I am feeling good, today," Madi replies. "I am trying to figure out what to do with my day."

"I may stop by for lunch," she says.

"That is fine," Liam replies. "I will not have much time to talk until later."

"I let you sleep, last night," Liam says. "You need your rest."

"Thank you, Liam," Madi replies. "Yes, I did rest well."

"I will see you, shortly," Madi says, "after the lunch rush."

"Sounds good, Madi," Liam says. "I miss you."

"I miss you, too," Madi replies.

Madi is getting comfortable with her role around Liam. It feels right for her, now. She is hoping and praying that Liam feels the same. They are still young in their relationship. Madi stands up from her chair. She puts her telephone in her purse. She looks through her purse to find her keys. She looks in the mirror at the front door. She looks fine. She wraps a warm coat around her and puts on her outside boots. Madi locks the door behind her.

Madi stops her car at the four-way stop at the end of her lane. She waves at Ron and Brenda. They are out for a morning walk. They smile back, and Madi makes a right turn.

Madi travels down the road. She wants to enjoy drive time alone in the car before starting her workday, tomorrow. She prays Liam will find another server, soon. She wants her old life back. Four days each week is enough. Madi hopes to talk to Liam about this, today. She turns her radio on searching for soft music. Madi continues along the road.

Madi heads out of the city on a small, country road. She passes by farmhouses. She passes broken fences with beautiful homes behind them. Children are playing in the yard. "*Those days are gone*," Madi thinks to herself. It is adult years now. She has so many choices to make each day.

Madi has travelled far enough. It is time to turn around and head back to Nucton. She is getting hungry. Madi needs a coffee refill.

Madi passes the children playing in the yard, the homes, the broken fences along the same winding road. Madi comes back to the highway and turns towards the city. She continues.

Madi heads straight to the diner and soon arrives. The parking lot is near empty, only a couple of cars on the far end of the parking lot.

Madi parks in her usual spot. She locks the car doors behind her. Madi walks through the front door.

Liam greets her with a smile, a hug, and a gentle kiss on the cheek.

Madi blushes. Customers are sitting at the tables finishing their lunch.

"I will grab a seat," Madi says. "I would like a garden salad and a ginger ale."

Madi finds her seat at the staff table.

Liam brings her a ginger-ale. "The salad will be a few minutes," Liam says.

Liam heads back to the kitchen. He is back in five minutes with her salad and a couple of salad dressing choices.

"I will leave you to lunch," Liam says. "I hope I can find a few minutes to talk."

"Me, too," Madi replies. Madi goes back to her lunch.

The diner is soon empty. Liam has time to sit down with Madi. He joins her at the staff table.

Liam apologizes for the past week.

"I am working too much," Madi says. "I do not have enough time for myself."

"I am working on it," Liam says. "Be patient."

"The last couple of weeks have been rough on me," Madi replies.

"We do need more staff in here," Madi says. "Four days each week is enough for me."

Liam is surprised at how forward Madi is with him. He does not expect it from her.

"Is everything ok, Madi?" Liam asks.

"I need time for me," Madi replies. "There have been so many changes for me to digest."

Madi and Liam are learning each other's limits. Liam has reached his, and now Madi has reached hers.

"I do understand," Liam says. "I will be hiring by the end of the week."

"I appreciate it," Madi says. "I do want to go to college."

"I understand," Liam replies.

"Our relationship has been on hold," Madi says.

"Work and life balance is very important to me," Madi says. "We need a life outside of this place if we are going to make it."

Madi is straight forward. She knows what she needs. She is still struggling with the changes. She has still not decided what she wants from life. Madi needs good people in her life that can help her find it.

Liam has been selfish. He hopes and prays he is the right one to find what Madi is missing in her life.

Madi finishes her lunch. "I should get going, Liam," Madi says.

"What time do you want me in, tomorrow?" she asks.

"Eight o'clock is good," Liam says. "I will have the new schedule on the wall."

"Thank you, Liam," Madi replies.

Madi heads towards the door. She has tears in her eyes. She hopes she has not been too hard on Liam. Madi hopes more that her mother is wrong about Liam. She wants Liam to be the right one for her life. They have so many years together. It will be a shame to let it all slip away if they cannot work things out.

Madi drives home in quietness.

Eighteen

Madi arrives at the diner at seven forty-five to prepare for her day. She checks the schedule. Liam has Madi scheduled for four days the next two weeks. She smiles and sits down to enjoy her coffee. Madi leaves her coffee on the staff table. Customers begin to arrive. She washes up and greets them with a smile.

"Good morning, how many seats do you need?" Madi asks the cordial question, every morning.

It will take, Madi, time to get back into a regular routine. She gets through her day with a smile on her face. The breakfast rush is the usual, mostly her regulars. They are always happy to see her. Madi, too, is happy to see them.

They thank her and gift her well with tips every day. She has a small break before the lunch rush, and then again, a longer break between lunch and dinner. In the latter period she would go home for a couple of hours if the work was done. She uses those few hours to organize her house. Other times she would just put her feet up. Madi would arrive back to the diner in time for the dinner rush.

Liam greets her with a smile. "I hired a new gal," Liam says. "She is starting tomorrow."

"Her name is Becky," Liam speaks firmly. "I am counting on you to show her the routine."

"Of course," Madi replies.

"In a week or two," Liam says. "I am hoping we can manage regular days with no split shifts."

"Wow, I cannot wait," Madi replies. "We can have a have a life outside of here, again."

"It is going to take real effort on all of our part to make this work," Liam says.

"I would like to take you out on Saturday night," Liam says changing the topic.

"Would you like to go to the other diner, again?" he asks with a hint of laughter in his voice.

Madi looks up at Liam, "I would like that," Madi replies. "It was a great night."

Madi leaves the diner smiling. The drive home is quiet. It is dusk when she arrives at her front door. It is the usual routine at home. Madi is glad to be in the comfort of her little nest. She reads a little in a warm bath. Madi is in bed early with the lights out.

The next couple of days are a normal routine for Madi. She goes through business as usual. Madi is happy when Friday night arrives. She watches a little TV before heading to bed.

Madi and Liam work the Saturday shift through the lunch hour. Liam has already posted the closure on the door for the evening. Madi cannot believe all of this is happening.

Madi closes the kitchen. It is ready for Sunday morning. She drives home in quietness with a beautiful smile. Madi arrives home with only enough time to shower. She freshens up before Liam arrives at her door.

Madi is more comfortable with him every day at her home. She feels her youth, again. They laugh together. They talk through dinner.

Liam drives her home. He waits in the truck until Madi speaks.

Madi turns to Liam. "Would you like to come in for a visit?" she asks.

Liam nods. He does want to come in for a little bit. He has barely seen Madi in the last few weeks. He wants more out of life for them, too.

Madi unlocks the front door and sees them both inside. She locks the door behind him. She takes his coat and hangs it up in the closet. Madi plugs the kettle in to prepare the tea.

"The den is more comfortable," she says. "I will bring the tea in."

"You are domestic, my friend," Liam comments looking around the home.

"Thank you," Madi replies.

"I like things in order," Madi says. "I hope you feel at home."

"Very much, Madi," Liam says. "Your home is lovely."

Madi arrives with the teapot, setting it carefully on the tea table. She returns to the kitchen for the other items. She sits down in the chair next to Liam.

"I will let it steep for a bit," Madi says. "Mom says it is best not to serve your guests weak tea, like dish water."

"What else does your mother say, Madi?" Liam asks.

"Why would you ask that?' Madi asks.

"I was just saying," Liam speaks with a laugh.

"For a quiet little church girl, Madi," Liam speaks with a chuckle. "You do know yourself."

"You have quite a wit, miss," Liam says. "I love it, because I do love you."

"I love you, too, Liam," Madi replies. "I do not know how we got here."

Madi stands up and pours two cups of tea. She pours milk in each cup. She hands one to Liam.

Madi sits down across from him with her tea in hand.

"All I have to do is get creditability with your mother," Liam sighs.

"Will I ever win her trust?" he asks.

"I think you will in time," Madi says. "First, we need to win each other."

"Our high school years were pretend love," Madi replies. "I am tired of pretending, Liam."

"Me, too," Liam replies.

Liam finishes his tea and Madi, too. Liam breaks the silence.

"It is getting late," Liam says. "I should be heading home."

Madi walks him to the door and hands him his coat. "It has been a beautiful evening," she says.

Liam is looking in her eyes. Madi does not back away, nor does she blush. Liam pulls her close and holds her in his arms. "Thank you, for waiting for me," Liam says. He kisses her on the lips.

Madi kisses him back. Her heart is racing. This is the beginning for Madi and Liam.

Nineteen

Sunday morning is quiet at the diner. Madi looks after her business and Liam tends to his. She finishes her morning coffee. She prepares the breakfast buffet before people arrive. Liam walks by leaving the kitchen. He smiles at her. Madi smiles back. The morning is off to a good start. Cars are pulling up to the diner. Madi needs to keep herself composed. She has a long day to get through. Her heart is full.

Madi greets people at the door walking each of them to their seats. She places their orders and shows them to the buffet. Sundays are usually busy. They have one of the better brunches in the city. Her duties of the day come and go. The day is ending.

Madi cannot wait to get home. She is inspired to cook a nice dinner, tonight.

Liam interrupts her thoughts. "What are you thinking, dear?" Liam asks. "I see a beautiful smile."

"I am happy," Madi says. "I am going home to cook a nice dinner for me."

"You can join me later," Madi says. "I am going to pick up salmon on the way home."

Liam thinks about it. "I can probably be convinced," he replies.

"What can I bring?" Liam asks.

"Whatever you feel, Liam, maybe a dessert, whip cream and fruit will be nice," Madi replies.

"Would you like a glass of wine with dinner?" Liam asks.

"If you like," Madi replies, "you know I do not drink."

"One glass will not hurt," Liam says. "It is a glass of wine, Madi!"

Madi ignores the thought and grabs her coat.

"Goodbye, Liam," Madi says. "Come by around seven-thirty."

Liam kisses her goodbye. "I look forward to seeing you, later," Liam replies.

Madi smiles up at him. She walks out the door and heads straight home. She makes a quick stop at the grocery store to pick up the things she needs for dinner. Madi arrives home and puts the groceries in the fridge. She runs upstairs and jumps in the shower. She freshens up before her dinner preparations. She pulls a bright, red sweater over her head. She puts on her pair of gray dress pants. Madi put on a little hint of mascara with a little eyeshadow. Madi touches herself up with a little perfume.

Madi is back to the dinner menu, a simple and natural touch. The rice is in the rice cooker. The vegetables are in the steamer ready to turn on as Liam arrives. She rinses the salmon and places it on a plate. She dusts them with a little olive oil and finishes them with a dash of salt and pepper. Madi covers the fillets and puts them back in the fridge. She sets the dining room table. She fluffs the linen and changes the placemats to color match. She finds her best cutlery pieces and napkins. Madi laughs, she is becoming her mother.

The table is set. She has time to relax before Liam arrives. Madi grabs her Bible and sits at the other end of the table. She prays:

Heavenly Father

I do not know everything that you are doing in my life.
I do ask you to show me as I need to know.
Please prepare me for the future that you have for me.

Amen

Madi opens her Bible, and it falls open to Psalm 34. Madi finds comfort in the words in front of her.

Madi looks up. She hears Liam's truck pull into the driveway. She unlocks the front door.

Liam walks inside and removes his footwear.

Liam kisses Madi. "I just feel it, Madi," Liam says. "If it is too much, please let me know."

"It is all good," Madi says taking his coat and hanging it in the closet.

Liam walks by and sees the neatly set table.

"Wow, pretty fancy here," Liam says. "I am going to put the wine and dessert in the fridge."

"I know you are not much for wine," Liam says. "I thought a little wine might be nice."

Madi moves around the kitchen, quickly. She turns on the rice cooker. It will take a bit more time than the fillets. She and Liam retire to the den. They talk and share for quite a time. The time passes. She needs to put the fillets on. Madi excuses herself.

Liam nods his approval.

"I really appreciate tonight," Liam says. "Next weekend, dinner is at my place."

"I can put chicken on the BBQ," Liam replies.

"That sounds great," Madi replies happy to be sharing real life with someone that she loves.

Liam is a good man. They have seen each other through struggles. Madi cannot see herself with another man. She knows he is the one for her. It feels right.

Madi cooks the salmon through. The rice is ready. Madi serves both their plates and sets them on the table.

Liam pours himself a glass and wine, and Madi, too.

Madi has two glasses of water set on the table.

Madi takes Liam's hand. She blesses the food and thanks God for the day.

"Amen," Liam says.

Madi looks at him and smiles.

"It looks great, Madi," Liam says.

"Where did you learn to cook?" he asks.

"Some from my mother but mostly I learned on my own," Madi says.

"I like simple meals," Madi replies.

"I am not much for sugar and sauces on the food," she replies. "I like my food natural."

"This dinner is great," Liam says. "Thank you for letting me share a glass of wine at your dinner engagement."

"I know it is not your thing, Madi," Liam says.

Madi tries a sip of Liam's wine. It tastes bitter.

"Liam, I think I will leave it with you," she replies.

"That is ok, Madi," Liam says. "Please forgive me."

Madi just smiles and let it go. She is being patient with him as he learns more about her. Madi knows she needs to be strong all the way. Madi is choosing God's way.

Madi cannot wait for the day when Liam is ready to be the spiritual leader.

"Dinner was lovely, Madi," Liam says. "Thank you, again."

"You are welcome, Liam," Madi replies.

Madi lay the dishes in the sink. She will wash them, later.

Madi and Liam retire to the den for conversation and dessert. They both look at each other and laugh while eating their dessert.

"It is lovely, Liam," Madi says. "It is an excellent choice."

"It is right from my kitchen," Liam laughs.

"I cannot take credit for this one," Liam corrects his humor. "The local bakery down the road did it."

"Thank you," Madi replies. "It is a nice touch to the end of the dinner."

"Liam, thank you," she says, "for everything you have given me."

"I enjoy working for you," Madi replies. "You are a wonderful boss."

"I the same with you," Liam replies. "You are a great employee."

"Enough, shop talk," Liam says. "I do not want to have to fire you."

"This is not official, Madi," Liam says. "You are the woman I want to marry."

Madi does not know what to say. "It is something we can work towards," she replies.

"Do you think it is time to talk with your parents?" Liam asks.

"If you feel it is the right time," Madi speaks. "I am behind you."

"I am a little nervous around your mother," Liam says, "to be honest." "She scares me."

"Take her as you see it, Liam," Madi says. "She is not happy."

"I am sorry to hear that," Liam says.

"I need to be strong to deal with it, Liam," Madi says. "I cannot make her happy."

"I tried for many years," Madi says.

"I choose to be happy, every day," Madi replies.

"I do miss my conversations with Brent," Madi says. "I remember the games he plays, too."

"I had to let them go," Madi says. "I pray for them when they are on my heart."

"My family is easy going," Liam says. "I am sorry."

"We do not live with each other," Liam says. "We still enjoy each other when we get together."

"We help each other out when someone needs it," he says.

"Let's wait for a few weeks," Liam replies. "We should make a dinner date with your mom and dad."

"That sounds good," Madi says. "We can show them a fun night at our favorite place."

"It is getting late," Liam says. "I am working tomorrow, and you are off the schedule."

"Enjoy your day off, Madi," Liam says. "I will see you, Tuesday."

Madi walks Liam to the door.

Liam kisses her good night.

Madi kisses him back.

Madi locks the door behind Liam. She turns all the lights on the main floor off. Madi heads upstairs.

It has been a long day. She crawls into bed.

Madi falls sleep.

Twenty

Madi wakes up thankful the day is Monday. She does not have to get out of bed. She rises, anyway. She dresses quickly, has a bite to eat and is out the door. Christmas is coming. She still has preparations for the day and gifts to buy. Madi decides today will be a good day to look after her shopping list. She is off to the mall. Madi arrives at the mall a little early. She stops by the drive thru and grabs herself a coffee. Madi sips her coffee and enjoys a quiet time in the car with the radio playing, softly. She enjoys every part of the moment. It is fifteen minutes until the doors open. The grocery store is open. Madi drives in the new direction. She grabs the things she needs for the week.

Madi shuffles her groceries around in the trunk of her car. She is off to do the rest of her Christmas shopping. She goes through the list: Liam, Brent, dad, mom, Doris, Ron, and Brenda. *"It is enough,"* she thinks to herself. She wants to find a chain for Liam; Ron and Brenda something to share for the house, and mom and dad, too and Brent. Doris, she will have to decide at the end. Madi thought jewelry to be appropriate.

Madi walks the mall until the noon hour. She is hungry. She stops for lunch at the mall. Her arms are full of parcels. She sets them down. Madi rests and eats her lunch.

Madi is loading her parcels in the trunk. She hears a voice behind her. It is Liam. She turns to greet him. She is standing between the parcels and looks in his eyes. "What are you up to?" Madi asks.

"We ran out of a few things at the diner" Liam replies. "I have to run." He whispers something, quietly.

Madi does not understand his whispers. She does understand his smile, though. Madi chuckles, on the way home. She knows he loves her.

Madi arrives home and parks the car. She unloads the parcels and groceries and leaves them at the front door. She closes the trunk and locks the car doors. Madi is walking up the steps. She turns around hearing Brenda's voice.

"Hello, Madi," Brenda whispers.

"Hi," Madi replies.

"Stop by for tea, later," Brenda says.

"I would like that, very much," Madi replies. "I will put away my groceries and Christmas parcels."

"I will be over, shortly," Madi says.

"Sounds good," Brenda replies.

Madi has her stuff all sorted and put away. She is having a beautiful day.

Madi is off to see Brenda. Madi rang the doorbell.

Brenda is close to the door. She opens the front door.

"Welcome, Madi," Brenda says. "Come on in."

"Hello, young lady," Ron says smiling over his newspaper. "Please join us for a tea, biscuits, and jam."

Madi removes her shoes and sets them on the mat and hands her jacket to Brenda. She follows Brenda into the kitchen. Brenda seats her at the back of the table. Ron sits at the head of the table. Brenda to his right. The teapot is on the table with all the fixings, including the biscuits and jam.

Ron looks at Madi. "What have you been up to?" Ron asks. "You look rested."

"It has been a good week for me, at least," Madi replies. "I am on a regular schedule."

"Good for you, Madi," Ron says.

"I am blessed," Madi replies.

"I have time to keep up with my life," Madi says. "I like to live, too."

"Balance is important," Ron replies.

"My poor feet and mind," Madi says.

"Oh," Brenda says. "Would you like to share?"

"Liam and I have grown beyond our friendship," Madi continues. "I am possibly looking into further education."

"Good for you," Brenda replies.

"Liam has even made mention of selling the diner," Madi replies, "and educating, further himself."

"Do your parents know all of this?" Ron asks.

"Not yet," Madi replies. "It is part of our plans."

"Liam thinks it is best to deal with it over a nice dinner with my parents," Madi says. "It all needs to happen before Christmas."

"Christmas is only a couple of weeks away!" Brenda says.

"Yes, I know," Madi replies. "I just finished my shopping, today."

"Good for you," Brenda replies laughing. "I have not!"

"I have to do it when I am thinking about it," Madi says. "My schedule can change every week."

"Are you thinking about a nine to five job, Madi?" Ron asks.

I need to do what fits me," Madi replies, "and choose from there."

"I want my education to be a good fit, nothing wasted," Madi says. "I want to like what I do."

"Wisdom and planning are good," Ron replies. "We spend many hours in a workplace."

"There are things you can plan with good choices," Ron says. "There will always be stuff that is out of your own control." "It is the world we are living in."

"We need a good paycheck to cover our ever-growing costs and some to enjoy life, too," Ron says.

"Thank you, Ron," Madi says. Ron and Brenda are like second parents to Madi.

"After dinner with your parents," Ron says. "Please bring Liam over to meet us."

"I will do that," Madi says. "I should be heading home."

"Thank you, again," she says.

Madi arrives home and locks the door. She removes her shoes and jacket.

It is close to the dinner hour. Madi is not hungry. She has eaten all day. Madi enjoys the rest of her evening before her workday, tomorrow. She is hoping Liam will call this evening. She sits in the comfort of her front room chair enjoying a good book from her own bookshelf. Madi is well into the third chapter when the telephone rings.

Madi grabs her telephone. It is Liam.

"Good evening, Madi," Liam speaks first.

"How was your day?" he asks.

"It was great," Madi replies.

"I went to the mall, came home, had tea with Ron and Brenda," Madi says. "I just got home an hour ago and have been reading my book."

"Sounds like you had a good day," Liam replies.

"I am still at the diner," Liam says.

"It is all wrapped up here," Liam replies. "I am heading home soon."

"I am glad you called me," Madi says.

"I want you in my life," Liam says. "I want a future with you."

"I want you in my life, too, Liam," Madi replies. "I cannot do it alone, anymore."

"I have your back," Liam says, "like the good old days."

"We are in life together," he says, "for the long haul." Madi does not know what to say.

Liam says it for her, "Good night, hon, talk tomorrow."

Good night, Liam," Madi replies and hangs up the telephone.

Madi goes right to bed. She falls asleep.

Twenty-One

Madi goes through her day's duties, business as usual.

At home, she spends her time researching potential opportunities that may be of interest to her future. Madi does not want to make this decision alone. It is a bigger financial commitment than she can bear. She likes the idea of becoming a teacher. It is honorable. She knows it is a tough study with a big commitment. She wants to serve. Madi set it all aside until she can discuss it further with Liam. He needs to be with her on this one.

The next few days will go by quickly. She and Liam finally find time for each other on Saturday night.

Liam picks her up promptly at six o'clock. They stop at a small Chinese restaurant and share their weeks happenings together. They share a dinner for two with a pot of jasmine tea. Liam breaks the silence.

"How was your week?" Liam asks.

"It was eventful," Madi replies. "I have so much to tell."

"I do not know where to start," Madi says. "We should meet with my parents."

"Yes," he says.

"Any idea where we should take them?" he asks.

"They do not go out, much," Madi says. "We could take them to the Italian place, downtown."

"That sounds good, Quito's, right!" Liam says.

"Do you want to arrange it together, Madi?" Liam asks.

"Yes, I would like that," Madi says.

"What time do they go to bed at night?" Liam asks.

Madi has an intrigued look on her face. "Usually, after nine o'clock or nine-thirty," Madi replies.

"Come by my place for a late dinner, tomorrow," Liam says.

"We will call them after dinner," he replies.

"That sounds good," Madi says, "maybe next Saturday night for dinner with my parents."

"Yes," Liam says. "Saturday nights are best for us."

"I have made my best decision on school," Madi says.

"It is too expensive and with work and study balance," Madi replies. "It does not seem right."

"You are correct, Madi," Liam says. "It is a big decision to make on your own."

"Thank you for telling me," Liam says.

"You do not have to do anything you are not comfortable with," Liam speaks.

"Thank you, Liam," Madi says with a smile.

"A teacher is more to my liking," Madi says.

"One thing at a time," Liam replies, "it is almost Christmas." "Let's enjoy some family time, this month."

Madi does not want to discuss it anymore.

"I finished my Christmas shopping the other day, did you?" Madi asks.

"No, I am a man," Liam replies laughing. "We all line up on Christmas Eve."

Madi knows he is joking. "No," Madi replies. "I will not do your shopping."

"It is ok," Liam says.

"I have a list," he says. "Santa will do it for me."

"Do not give me the Santa is not real story," Liam replies. "You will crumble my whole childhood."

"I will not dare," Madi says.

"I will clearly mark my gifts," she says with a smile. "Santa is not getting credit for mine."

"We have our differences," Liam says, "but I still love you." "We will deal with them one at a time."

"I love you, too, Liam," Madi replies.

"It has been a good evening," Liam says. "I enjoy our chats."

"There is a time to have fun," Liam says. "And a time to be responsible."

Madi yawns, "I am tired, Liam," she says.

"It is getting late," Liam speaks.

Madi follows him to the front, and he pays the bill. They walk out the door together. He helps her in the passenger side of the truck. They arrive at Madi's door. Liam parks the truck. He helps Madi out of the truck. He walks her to the door and kisses her good night. He waits while she locks the door behind her.

Liam drives home in quietness, tonight. He is tired, too. He will be in bed, soon. It has been another long week for both, Madi and Liam. He does not want Madi in school, right now. The economy is not stable, and he fears it may take them out of Nucton. They will have to pray about it and then decide what is right for them.

Liam is practical, and so is Madi. They will choose what is right.

Twenty-Two

Madi wakes up Sunday morning. There is a little snow on the road. She is heading to Liam's house for dinner after work. Madi has slept in later than usual.

Liam will open the diner, this morning.

Madi jumps in the shower. She dresses in her work clothes. She grabs a banana for her pocket and slips her winter coat over her shoulders. She ties her shoes and is on the road. The music is quiet, and she is singing softly. It is her moment of church each Sunday morning. She enjoys the hymn sing that plays on the radio each Sunday morning. It encourages her and gives her strength. Madi does not enjoy working Sundays, it goes with the job. She just does it.

Madi arrives at the diner. She parks the car and locks the doors. Madi is five minutes late. She hopes Liam will give her time for a coffee before the day begins.

Madi walks through the front door.

"Good morning, Madi," Liam says. "Grab a coffee, you have ten minutes before anyone arrives."

"Thank you," Madi smiles.

It is her first coffee, today. She pours herself a cup and walks to the staff table. Madi sits down and enjoys every sip. Sunday brunch is a busy time. She finishes her coffee, and the customers start to arrive. She is on her feet at the door before she is asked. She greets every guest the same with a smile. Madi seats them all. She is careful to please each new face and every regular that she meets. Madi offers them a coffee. She continues with her regular rounds. She takes their orders and sends them off to the buffet.

Today is a busy, Sunday. They will be cleaning up and heading home, soon.

Madi and Liam do not have time to talk. They are both glad when the end of the day arrives.

Liam closes early. They are out the door by seven o'clock.

"Thank you for everything," Liam says.

"Follow me home," Liam replies. "Dinner will not take long to prepare."

"Let's telephone mom and dad, first thing," Madi says. "Then we can both relax!"

"A good idea!" Liam replies. "I am training Becky, tomorrow."

"She has some great experience," Liam says. "I am hoping for a couple of days to get her up to our standards."

"Cool! Madi replies. "An extra set of reliable hands will help us all."

"I am hoping and praying," Liam says.

Madi notices Liam is praying more often. She trusts it is real. Madi does not want to doubt. She knows he is on her side.

Liam is real.

She is thankful for the friends that she does have today. She has Liam, Ron, Brenda, and Doris. They are all good people. She is thankful for Liam, the most. She just wants him to know how serious her faith in God is. Madi's love for God comes first in her life.

Liam is in his truck. He pulls out of the driveway and is heading towards his home.

Madi follows close behind.

They both park in his driveway twenty minutes later. Madi follows Liam to the front door.

Liam unlocks the door and motions Madi inside, first. He is a gentleman. They walk inside. Liam locks the door behind her. He smiles at Madi. He touches her lips with a kiss.

"Thank you for your help, today, Madi," Liam says.

"You are welcome," Madi replies.

Give me ten minutes to freshen up," Liam says. "We will call your parents."

Madi likes it when Liam is in charge. She sits in the parlor and waits patiently for him. She laughs.

"What is so funny? Liam asks.

"Nothing," she replies.

"Really," Liam replies. "You are blushing."

"I am sorry," Madi replies. "I must be expressing my thoughts out loud."

"Some days you are a mystery," Liam replies.

Liam will not change a thing about her. They have been friends for so long. There is nothing they can hide from each other.

"Let's call your parents!" Liam says.

"We can use the speaker on the land line," Liam says.

"I can manage the conversation."

Madi accepts.

Liam picks up the telephone and carries it to the front room. They share the sofa seat, together.

Madi nestles close to Liam on the sofa. He smiles at Madi, and she back at him.

"Are we ready? Liam asks.

"Yes," Madi replies.

Liam dials the number.

"Hello," mom says.

"Hello, Elisabeth," Liam replies.

"Hello, Liam," Elisabeth replies.

"I did not expect to hear from you," Elisabeth says. "Is Madi alright?"

"She is right here," Liam replies. "She is good."

"Hello mom," Madi says.

"Good to hear from you," Elisabeth replies. "Dad says hi."

"We have something to ask you," Madi says.

Liam nods for Madi to continue.

"Are you busy next Saturday night?" she asks.

"Not that we are aware of," mom replies.

"Liam and I would like to take you and dad for dinner at Quito's with Brent, too, of course," Madi says.

"I will have to discuss it with your father," mom says. "It should not be a problem."

"What is up?" Elisabeth asks.

"The usual," Madi replies. "There is something we want to talk about."

"Being Christmas, we thought we could celebrate it, too," she says.

"I suppose," mom says.

"Are you coming over for Christmas dinner?" mom asks.

"I have not made any plans for Christmas Day," Madi replies. "I would expect yes."

"Your dad is sleeping," mom replies. "We will get back to you tomorrow to confirm, Saturday."

"Good night, Madi," mom says. "Good night, Liam."

"Good night, mom," Liam says.

Liam hangs up the telephone.

"Relax, Madi," Liam says. "I will prepare dinner."

"Dinner is mostly prepared in the fridge," Liam replies. "It will not take more than twenty minutes."

"Sounds good, Liam," Madi replies. "I will be in the front room."

Madi falls asleep in the chair. It has been another long week.

Liam has dinner plates set at the table. He whispers in Madi's ear. He startles her.

"I am sorry to wake you," Liam says.

Madi gathers herself together.

"Maybe you should sleep in the spare room," Liam speaks to Madi. "I do not want you driving home."

Madi does not argue. She does not want to drive home. She eats her dinner and finishes with a glass of milk.

"Thank you, Liam," Madi says. "Dinner was lovely."

"I will grab you a t-shirt to sleep in," Liam says. "There are extra towels in the bathroom."

"They toiletries are in the shower caddy," Liam replies. "Help yourself."

"Thank you," Madi replies.

"I will not be far behind you," Liam says. "I will be cleaning up the kitchen, soon."

Liam finds a t-shirt on the top of the dryer and hands it to Madi.

Madi reaches for his hand. She puts her arms around him and holds him close. They kiss each other good night. Madi makes her way to the shower.

Liam heads back to the kitchen.

The lights are out in Madi's room.

Liam's room is not far behind.

The house is quiet.

Twenty-Three

Madi wakes to the sound of Liam's alarm. She forgets where she is. It is her day off.

Madi jumps into the shower to wipe the night from her body. She dresses.

Madi and Liam smile at one another.

Liam is making coffee for each of them.

Madi and Liam kiss each other and say their goodbyes.

Madi is on the road home, singing softly and sipping her coffee.

Madi arrives home. She has a full day to occupy, herself. She changes her clothes and throws the others in the laundry. She finishes her coffee and reads a little from her Bible. She thanks God for every good thing in her life.

Madi still wants to go to school, one day. Money is tight. Liam is right. She is grateful to have him in her life. She lays her thoughts aside. She finishes her coffee.

Madi is in her car with the music playing softly. She pulls off the driveway and moves onto the boulevard. Madi misses her turn on the main highway. She has a destination driving to the countryside. She needs to be alone to be close to God. The fresh air and singing birds remind her God's love is nearby. It is a reminder of all of God's promises. Madi wants to keep her heart and mind pure. Madi parks the car. She finds the most beautiful balm tree and walks under its protection. Madi prays.

Heavenly Father

I thank you for this life that you have given me.
I thank you for what you are doing in my life
and Liam's. God, if there be any unforgiveness in me,
I ask you to bring it to me that I can deal with it.
I ask you, God, to keep us in your right in this relationship.
I ask you, God, to keep this relationship pure all the days of our lives.
I ask you, God to keep people out of our life that are not to be there.
Take us step by step, in the path that you would like us to walk. God,
Show me the path of life, and education that you have for me in your time.

Amen

Madi lives for these moments in her life. She hopes and prays Liam will come to understand the need for a simple faith. The refreshing of the Holy Spirit sweeps over Madi's soul in these times.

These are the times God takes away all of her fears and worries. She trusts she can leave all her cares at the feet of Jesus.

Madi rises and sings the song that is stirring in her spirit.

Lord you are more precious than silver,
Lord you are more costly than gold,
and nothing I desire compares with you…

The words of this chorus sing in her heart, often. She remembers the words from her childhood. Madi has tears in her eyes. How far she has strayed over the years. She wants her comfort to be in her love for Jesus Christ. God is leading her back to comfort in him. It does not matter how she makes her living. God will take care of her every need.

Madi had a beautiful day. The drive home was as beautiful as the drive out. The soft music playing in the background. Madi's sweet voice humming and singing on the way home. She is grateful to God for all his goodness. She is thankful for Liam's love. She does not enjoy making all the decisions of the home. She is not a coward in God's eyes. It is the way God made her. Madi knows her strengths and weaknesses.

Madi pulls the car into her driveway. It is after three o'clock. She has enjoyed another beautiful day. She laughs to herself. She forgot to eat, today. Madi makes her way into the house. She does not want to ruin her dinner. She grabs an apple and a pudding from the fridge. She fills her water jug. She sits down at the table with a snack.

The telephone rings. It is her mother. Madi's mouth is full. She waits and dials the telephone when she is finished eating.

"Hello, mom," Madi speaks.

"Sorry I could not pick up the telephone, earlier," Madi says. "I was eating."

"Thank you for calling back, Madi," mom speaks. "Your dad has declined dinner out."

"You are welcome to come by Saturday for dinner," mom says.

"OK," Madi says. "I would like to bring Liam."

"I will have to see," mom replies. "You know how we feel about him."

"Liam is a big part of my life," Madi says.

"You should stop by, alone." mom says.

"Not without Liam," Madi says.

"When is the last time you went to church?" mom asks.

"Has Liam been to church with you?" mom asks.

"Mom," Madi says. "I am not going to discuss my personal life."

"You know your lifestyle is not as we raised you to choose," mom replies.

"I am an adult," Madi replies. "I am responsible and so is Liam."

"It is your choice," mom replies.

"Yes, it is," Madi replies.

"Then choose it," mom replies. "We believe you are making a big mistake with Liam."

"You do not know Liam," Madi replies. Madi ends the conversation.

"Goodbye, mom," Madi says. "I love you."

"We love you, too," mom replies, "goodbye."

Madi hangs up the telephone. She cries. Madi prays quietly. Her tears become joy. She is heartbroken from her mothers' rejection. She wants her approval.

Madi is struggling to accept this. She knows she needs to give it to God.

Madi waits to call Liam.

Madi knows only God's love is big enough to pull her through these moments.

Twenty-Four

It is past the dinner hour.

Madi calls Liam at the diner. "Hello Liam," Madi says.

"Will you be home soon?" she asks.

"I should be home around seven o'clock," he says. "I am hoping we can talk."

"Is everything ok, Madi?" Liam asks.

"I am fine," Madi speaks softly. "I want you to know I talked with mom, today."

"Ok," Liam says.

"Are the plans good?" he asks.

"No," Madi says.

"What time should I call?" she asks.

"Call me at nine o'clock," he says. "It gives me time to clean up and chill."

"Sounds good," Madi says and hangs the telephone.

Madi has time to herself. She surfs the TV. She finds nothing of interest to her. Madi decides a walk would be nice. She dresses warm. There is a white blanket of snow on the ground. The evenings are beautiful in Nucton. The temperature is perfect for a walk.

Madi steps onto the walkway and feels the crunch of hard, packed snow under her feet. She likes the sound under her boots. She would often find herself counting steps as she skips down the path. The glow of the light around the moon, and the sight of her breath in the night air is all she can see. The neighbors are tucked inside by the fireplace. Madi likes the outdoors, rain, snow, or shine. The sky is clear.

It is going to be a chilly morning. She can feel it. Winter is here, and Christmas time is near. The lights are out on all the streets. Madi reaches her destination, and her fingers and feet are cold. She turns around and walks back home.

Madi steps through the front door. She removes her shoes and outside clothes. Madi puts them away in the closet. She is careful to wipe the wet floor behind herself. It is time to call Liam. She jumps into the shower and makes herself comfortable for the night. The telephone rings. Madi left it on her bedside table. She is resting upright with her pillow behind her back. She leans over to read the number. It is Liam.

"Hello," she says with a smile. She is so happy to hear his voice.

"Hello," Liam says.

"How are you doing?" Liam asks. "Did it go well with your mother?"

"No," Madi replies. "They are not interested."

"I am so sorry," Liam replies. "I know how much it meant to you."

"I should be there Christmas Day," Madi replies. "I am not comfortable being there without you, anymore."

"I understand, Madi," Liam says.

"Am I invited?" he asks.

"No," Madi replies.

"I see," Liam replies. "We will pray about it."

"I do not want to go," Madi replies.

"I understand, Madi," Liam replies.

"I love you, Madi," Liam says.

"I love you, too," Madi replies.

"They are my parents," Madi says. "I want them to be happy for me."

"I wish I was there," Liam replies. "I could come by."

"I would like that," Madi replies. "I wish I was there with you."

"Be strong, Madi," Liam replies. "I will be there, soon."

"Would you like a coffee or a tea? Liam asks.

"I would like a hot tea," Madi replies, "with a little cream."

"Ok," Liam replies. He hangs up the telephone.

Liam heads over to Madi's house, soon after finishing the conversation.

Madi lay on her bed. She wants to cry. She stands up and straightens her composure.

Madi hears Liam's truck pull up. She waits.

Madi unlocks the front door. She opens the door to greet him. She smiles and kisses his cheek.

Madi takes the hot beverages from his hand and sets them on the table.

Liam takes off his outside clothes and lay them near the door. He takes her hand and holds her in his arms. He smiles at her and kisses her softly on the cheek.

"Thank you," Madi whispers.

They sit down on the sofa next to each other and sip their beverages.

Neither Madi, nor Liam speak.

Liam breaks the silence. "Would you like to get away for a couple of days for Christmas?' Liam asks.

"How can we do that with the diner?" she asks.

"We just do it," he says. "I can close the diner for a couple of days."

"I would like that," Madi replies.

"I will talk with Doris, tomorrow," Liam says. "If she is OK then consider it done."

"I will put a closed sign on the door for the twenty-fourth and twenty-fifth of the month," Liam continues.

"How does that sound?" Liam asks.

"Now, where do we go?" Madi asks with only a week away until Christmas.

"It is too cold to stay at the cabin," Liam says. "I will book a hotel away from here for a couple of nights."

Madi smiles at the thought, "I am in."

"I am in, too," Liam replies. "I should be going home."

"Let's pray together," he says putting on his boots and jacket. Liam stands up and faces Madi. He takes Madi's hand.

Madi smiles. "Go ahead," she replies.

Heavenly Father

I thank you for bringing us together in this time.

I ask you to bless this relationship every day that you give us together.
Teach us to walk in your ways as we choose to walk this life together.

Amen

Madi and Liam kiss each other good night.

Liam drives home.

Madi retires to her bedroom for the night.

Twenty-Five

Madi has been up waiting for Liam to call her in the late morning.

"Good morning, Madi," Liam speaks. "I hope your day is well."

"It is indeed," she replies. "You make me smile."

"It is confirmed," Liam speaks. "The closed signs are posted on the doors for the three days."

"Doris thinks it is an excellent idea," he replies. "She thinks we should do it every year."

"I am so excited," Madi replies.

"I booked a hotel with two rooms, for the twenty-third, twenty-fourth and twenty-fifth in Granum," Liam replies. "It is a couple hours' drive from here, weather permitting."

"There is a kitchen in the room," Liam continues. "We do not have to eat out every day."

"That sounds great," Madi replies.

"Doris wants our family get together to be in the new year," Liam speaks. "Go enjoy the rest of your day."

"I am off tomorrow," Liam replies. "I need to get back to work."

"Goodbye, Liam," Madi says. "I love you."

"I Love you, too," Liam replies. He hangs up the telephone.

Madi hangs up her telephone.

Madi is happy. She is tidying her modest home and catching up on the laundry. She did the grocery shopping, yesterday.

Madi retires to her room to read a book. She, later, takes a nap.

Christmas is soon approaching. Madi makes decisions for the things she needs to pack for the getaway. She sets it all aside. Tomorrow night they will head out after work. They decide to take Madi's car. It has a little more room. The luggage will keep dry in the backseat. Liam will drive. Madi makes the insurance coverage for him. She likes being prepared for emergencies. Madi calls her parents and let them know she will not be home for Christmas, this year. She will drop the gifts off when she arrives home. Liam agrees to take her over on Boxing Day. Her parents do not ask any questions. They wish her well.

The day arrives to head out. Madi's car is packed and fueled. They have taken inventory. They do not want to forget their essentials this time of year. They are tired from the workday. Yet, excited for the adventure. They grab a coffee for the road. There is no music only idle conversation and laughter along the way. Madi catches herself drifting off to sleep a couple of times. They make one stop to use the washroom and another for coffee.

They arrive late at their destination. There is parking. Liam checks in and picks up the keys.

Madi takes the luggage out of the car.

Later in the room, they set up their comfort zone for rest. Madi jumps in the shower first and then Liam. Liam sits down on Madi's bed and watches the TV. They soon turn in for the night and are asleep.

Madi and Liam wake near the same time, on Christmas Eve Day. They are anxious to get out and explore the town. They are hungry, too. Liam wants to find a lovely place for dinner, tonight and Christmas brunch. They decide on doing their gift exchange at dinner, tonight. Liam has others plans for tonight, too.

Madi and Liam hope to enjoy a walk, later, this evening.

They throw on their walking clothes and shoes. They want to stroll more than drive. They stop at a breakfast diner. They enjoy a breakfast of toast, eggs, and coffee. They are hoping to find someone at the diner that can share the town information with them. The staff are helpful long-time residents of the town. They have options for dinner, and parks close by. They finish breakfast and are back in the car to check out the town.

Madi and Liam find a lovely Italian café and agree it is more than enough for both dinner engagments. Liam makes reservations at seven o'clock for this evening. They reserve the table for Christmas brunch.

Madi and Liam are off to enjoy their day.

Liam takes the long route back to the hotel. It is a great way to see the town. They arrive back at the hotel and rest for an hour.

Madi and Liam wake up in time to freshen up for dinner. It will soon be time to leave for a festive dinner. Madi tucks Liam's gift into her purse. They lock the door behind them.

Madi and Liam are off to the little café. The café is only five minutes away. It is a quaint little place, comfortable and clean. It is the pick of many regulars. The décor is a red gingham tablecloth, square wood table and chairs, floral and candlelight. They arrive early and gracefully wait for a seat. They engage in conversation.

Madi and Liam are happy to be together this season.

Madi and Liam sit at a table in the corner near the fireplace. It is beautiful. There are stockings on the mantle. It is the feel of a beautiful Christmas. Madi recollects childhood Christmas memories. She feels tears in her eyes. Memories that are gone. It is time to make new memories.

Liam looks up at her. "Is everything ok?" he asks.

"I am just recollecting some of times gone," she replies. "It is time to create new memories."

"Amen, to that," Liam replies.

"Are you ready to order?" Liam asks.

"Yes, I am ready," Madi replies. "I would like the rainbow trout dinner."

"Sounds good," Liam says. "I believe I will have the same."

"Let's order," Liam speaks.

The server sees Liam nod and heads over to the table. He smiles and fills their water glasses. He places their orders and offers them a bottle of red wine. Liam looks at Madi for affirmation.

Madi declines and Liam, too.

The server nods and understands.

Madi and Liam engage in more conversation as they wait. They smile at each other. They are happy and grateful for this time together. Dinner arrives, trout fillets, roast potatoes, and steamed vegetables. How lovely it is. The server touches up their plates with salt and pepper. The server leaves them to enjoy their evening together.

They enjoy every bite and the quiet moments together. The server arrives in time to remove their plates. He fills their coffee mugs at their request.

Madi pulls Liam's gift from her purse and lays it on the table. Liam does the same.

"Are we ready?" Liam asks.

"Yes," Madi replies. She passes Liam his gift. "You go first."

Liam receives the package. He opens the little package. Inside the small box he finds the most beautiful gold locket. Inside the locket is a picture of Madi. The chain is strong enough to bear his workdays. He does not hesitate to remove it from the box. He puts it around his neck.

"It is beautiful, Madi," Liam says. He stands up and kisses her gently on the cheek.

"Thank you, my love," Liam speaks looking into her eyes.

"Now it is your turn," Liam replies. "I have something to ask you."

"Please look at me when you open the box," Liam says. He hands her the even smaller box.

Madi accepts the box. She does as Liam tells her. She opens the box to find the most beautiful solitaire diamond she has ever seen. She looks up at Liam with tears in her eyes.

"Do you like it?" Liam asks.

"What is not to like about it," she replies.

"Will you wear it?" he asks.

"Yes," Madi says.

Liam stands up from his chair and walks over to where Madi is sitting. He takes her hand and sits down low to make eye contact. Madi is blushing.

"Will you marry me, Madi?" Liam asks. Now he is perspiring. He knows she is the one he wants to spend the rest of his life with.

Madi looks at him with tears in her eyes. "Yes," she replies. She, too, knows this is the man she wants to spend the rest of her life with.

Liam takes the ring from the box and places it on her ring finger. They smile and Liam kisses her gently on the mouth.

Twenty-Six

Madi and Liam sit up and enjoy Christmas Eve in their hotel room. They are drinking hot cocoa and watching TV. It is mostly background noise. They talk for hours of their past and their future dreams. They fall asleep in each other's arm.

Madi awakes as Liam stirs around three o'clock in the morning. Madi retires to the comfort of her own bed until the sun shines bright in the room.

It is late Christmas Day. They have no plans. It is a day to relax. A drive around the countryside of Granum after brunch will be nice.

Granum is near closed today. They hope to find a coffee place even a truck stop open. Liam drives the car back to the husky station. He fills the car with fuel. They have a couple of hours before brunch at the café. They only want a place to sit and have a coffee. They grab a coffee and take it back to the room.

Soon it will be time to head to the café for brunch.

Madi and Liam arrive at the café, later in the day. A man is sitting alone at a table in front of them.

"Merry Christmas!" Liam says.

"Merry Christmas!" the man replies.

"Would you like to join us?" Liam asks. "Christmas is not a time to be alone."

Liam offers the man a seat and smiles. He is happy to share their table.

"What is your name?" Liam asks. "I am Liam and this is my fiancé, Madi."

"My name is Anthony," the man replies.

"I stop by for a hot meal," Anthony says, "when I can afford it."

"It has been a rough road this year," Anthony replies.

"Is there anything we can do to help," Liam says. "We are not rich but we work hard."

Madi and Liam order from the brunch menu.

Anthony continues with his story.

Madi feels tears roll down her cheek.

Madi turns to Liam, and Liam to Madi.

"Can we pray for you?" Liam says.

Madi smiles.

Anthony nods, affirmative.

Liam reaches for Anthony and Madi's hand, and Madi for Anthony. They bow their heads.

Liam prays aloud.

Heavenly Father

We thank you for this man. We ask you to heal his broken heart.
We ask you to bring your love and joy into his heart and life.
We ask for your provisions to abound this day and moving forward.

Amen

"We have your brunch," Liam says.

Madi and Liam finish their breakfast and pay their bill and Anthony's, too. They bless him. They are on their way. It is time for a drive in the countryside.

Liam contacted Doris, yesterday. He asked her to close the diner on Boxing Day, indicating they had family events to manage.

Liam takes a winding road out of the town of Granum. It is like most of the roads in British Columbia. It is snow covered all the way, filled with barns, corrals, farmhouses and broken fence posts to see. The sun is bright, and the sky is blue. There is not a cloud in the sky. It took a little longer to reach the hotel. They arrive in time for a nap.

They are ready to go home. It has been a good Christmas.

Madi wakes from her nap, first. She has a shower. Madi wakes up Liam. It is time for him to rise, anyway.

Madi prepares her things for an early rise tomorrow.

Liam has his shower. He, too, gathers his things for an early departure.

Bed is early, tonight. They will be up around six o'clock and on the road, the latest by seven o'clock. It is always the same protocol. They will grab a fresh coffee and be on the road home.

Six o'clock came early. They are both up and at it, promptly, eager for the events of the new day.

Madi and Liam are both rested. They laugh and sing on the trip home. Liam admits Madi has a much better tone than he does. They make a bathroom stop along the way, fill up their coffee mugs and are back on the road.

Liam pulls up to Madi's driveway in the early morning.

Madi grabs her bags and unlocks the front door of the house.

Liam carefully places his bag in the passenger side of his truck. He locks the truck door and follows Madi into her home.

Madi has the coffee pot on. She has breakfast cereal and milk on the table. Th fruit bowl has many options, too.

"This is breakfast, today," she smiles.

"It looks fine to me," Liam replies.

They eat together.

"We should call your parents and find out the best time to arrive," Liam says.

Madi calls her mother.

Madi's mom answers the telephone. "Merry Christmas," Elisabeth replies.

"Merry Christmas," Madi replies.

"What time can I stop by with your gifts?" she asks.

"We are home all day," Elisabeth says. "Any time after one o'clock."

"Two o'clock," Madi replies. "Liam is driving me over."

"OK," Elisabeth says. "I love you, Madi."

"I love you, too," Madi says.

"Goodbye, see you soon." She hangs up the telephone.

Liam heard the conversation. "I do not sound invited," he speaks. "I would like to go with you."

"I want you to come with me," Madi replies.

Madi and Liam move to the front room with their coffee mugs. They make themselves comfortable on the sofa.

Liam reaches for the TV remote. He thinks he might find a movie. At the least, good music for background noise. He settles on jazz tunes that they both agree on. It is Madi that breaks the silence.

"I have to accept it as it is," Madi speaks.

"Yes," Liam replies. "And we each live our own lives."

"I am tired of the emotional roller coaster," Madi says.

"Me too," Liam replies.

"Yes," Madi replies.

"It will be fine," Liam says. "Let's go for a walk."

Madi and Liam dress for the cool temperature. They put their gloves on. Madi locks the door behind them. She tucks her keys in her deep jacket pockets. She takes Liam's hand. They start their walk down the front walk along the walking path. Madi shows him her regular walk. They talk back and forth. The air is chilly. They are thankful for their gloves and the heat of each other's warmth in the clasp of their hand.

The fresh air feels good. It clears the mind and brings joy. They walk for a time. Madi's feet began to feel the chill. She decides it is time to head back to the house. Madi runs on ahead. It helps to warm her feet.

Madi and Liam have walked a little farther than a normal day in the cold. Liam catches up to Madi. They reach the front door of the house, together. Madi unlocks the door and lets them both inside. Her boots come off, first. She puts the kettle on, and then puts her boots and jacket away in the closet.

Liam tucks his boots away, next to the door and lay his jacket over the boots.

Madi makes a pot of tea and sets it on the kitchen table. She gathers the family gifts and sets the box at the front door.

Madi and Liam sit and enjoy a cup of tea together before they head out.

"It looks like it is time to go," Liam says. "I will drive."

Madi agrees. "Please and thank you," she replies.

Liam has his coat and boots on. He grabs the box from Madi. He carries it out and places it in the backseat of the car. He helps Madi into the car and kisses her on the cheek.

She smiles at him and whispers the words, "I love you."

Liam smiles back at her, "ditto."

They are on the road in Madi's car.

Madi breaks the silence. "We should pray," she says.

"Would you pray?" she asks.

"I can lead the prayer," Liam says. "And, you can finish."

"Sounds good," Madi replies.

Liam prays

Heavenly Father

We thank you for your goodness this season.
And the opportunity to share with the ones we love.
We thank you for the time to spend with Madi's family, soon.
We ask you to bless this time together.

Amen

Madi prays

Heavenly Father

I thank you for Liam's love this season and the time we shared together.
We thank you for the opportunity to meet with Anthony, and we ask you to bless
his days. We ask you to bless our time today as we share with mom, dad, and Brent.

Amen

Liam pulls into the driveway. They walk up the pathway together. Liam is carrying the box of gifts.

Mom greets them at the front door. She is surprised to see the two of them standing in front of her.

"Come in," mom says smiling. "Merry Christmas!"

Dad is welcoming. He shakes Liam's hand.

Liam sets the box of gifts down on the floor.

Madi distributes one to each of them, appropriately. They thank Madi for their gifts and hug her. They ask them in for tea. Mother has pastries sitting out on the table.

Liam tries his best to feel comfortable. It is his first time at Madi's parents.

Madi opens her gifts and thanks her parents and brother, gracefully.

They stay for dinner by invite. It is leftovers from the day before.

Elisabeth is an excellent cook. It is no hardship.

Liam breaks the silence at the end of the meal.

"I apologize it comes after the fact," Liam says. "I do want to ask permission to marry your daughter, properly."

"I am a gentleman," Liam speaks.

"I have asked her to marry me," Liam says, "and she has accepted."

"I know you have not always approved of me as her ideal suitor," Liam speaks. "I can provide a good living for her, and I do love her."

Steven nods the affirmative, "Yes."

Madi's mother speaks. "Are you a Christian?" she asks.

"Yes, Elisabeth I am," Liam says. "I may not walk ideally in your doctrinal views, but I am still a believer in Jesus Christ."

"Madi and I choose to walk together in daily prayer and reading of the scriptures to prove ourselves unto God," Liam replies.

Elisabeth is still not convinced but agrees only as Madi chooses.

Liam has done his best. They will have to trust God for the rest.

"Thank you for dinner," Liam says. "I have to run."

"We both have to work tomorrow," Liam replies. "I need to get Madi home and myself, too."

Madi thanks Liam. "I cannot make her happy for me, Liam," Madi says.

"It is not your responsibility to make her happy," Liam says. "You need to make you happy."

"I am happiest when I am with you," Madi replies.

"It is because we love each other," Liam says.

"I love your character, your virtues, your smile and your ability to laugh at the trivial things," Liam says. "These are the things I love most about you."

"I love you the same," Madi replies.

"You are my best friend," Madi says. "You have always been there for me."

Liam drops Madi at her home. He walks her to the door.

"I do have to go home, now," Liam says. "I will see you tomorrow."

"I love you, Madi," Liam says.

"I love you, too, Liam," Madi replies.

Madi watches Liam drive away in his truck.

Twenty-Seven

Madi wakes up early this morning. The sun is shining through the clouds, and it is a cold. It is the twenty seventh day of December. Madi is back to work, today. She is happy to be back at her regular routine.

She walks into the diner with a glow on her face. She meets Liam at the door. They smile at each other. He kisses her good morning.

"I had a lovely Christmas," Madi says.

"I did, too," he speaks to her with a smile.

Liam pours them each a cup of coffee. They sit down at the staff table.

Doris is in the back preparing the breakfast. She joins them. "Welcome back to town, Merry Christmas," she says, "and congratulations."

"Thank you," Madi replies.

"It is about time you two did something." Doris says facing Madi. "Welcome to the family."

"I hope you will join us for our regular, New Year's gathering," Doris says.

"I would like that, very much," Madi replies.

"We have mellowed over the years," Doris smiles at her brother. "We are not quite as loud and obnoxious."

"I am not sure what you are referring to, my sister," Liam replies.

"Are we telling stories?" he asks.

"I have stories, too," he laughs.

"I suppose we all do," Doris replies. "I am happy for you both." Doris walks back into the kitchen.

Madi and Liam finish their coffee and are back on their feet. Customers are pulling up into the driveway.

Madi prepares the coffee and buffet area. She does a general tidy up, checks the washrooms and seats her customers. Her regulars are happy to see her. Becky will soon be joining her on the floor, this morning. After today, the two girls will not see much of each other. They will work opposite shifts. Madi will cover the mornings, and Becky the afternoons.

It is a typical day for Madi. The training went well. Becky picked up her routine and managed to do things well. She is happy to be working, too. They are not too many opportunities in Nucton, for woman. Madi is grateful every day for God's provisions.

It is not long before Madi is hanging up her apron for the day. Her cleaning is done. She says her goodbyes and is soon heading home for the evening.

Madi is working through the rest of the week. The schedule will soon have her working regular mornings. Madi will have the rest of the day to lead a normal life. She will soon have time to do the things she likes to do.

The festivities finish for the season. The evening with Liam's family will be coming soon. Doris will be hosting it at her home. She is the one that likes to cook and entertain. Doris likes to be the boss and Liam, too. Liam manages her well. He makes the decisions.

Madi admires this character in Liam.

Twenty-Eight

Madi welcomes the new year with Liam close beside her. They stay home. It is safer. They have dinner together at Madi's place. Madi and Liam roast a chicken with all the fixings. It is a quiet dinner. They play cribbage until their eyes hurt. They wish each other Happy New Year.

"Are we spending New Year's Eve like old people?" Madi asks with a smile turning to look at Liam.

"We are not old, Madi," he replies with a laugh. "We are mature."

"OK," she laughs. "I had fun!"

"It is past my bedtime," she replies.

"Me too," he says. Liam knows he is crashing on the sofa tonight. "Good night, Madi."

Madi grabs him a pillow and an extra blanket. She leaves it on the sofa. Madi heads back up to her own room and crawls into her own bed. She lay on her bed. Madi can hear him walking around the kitchen, stumbling in the dark. He trips over something. She drifts off to sleep.

Liam tosses, turns, and nurses his toe. He gets up a couple of times in the night to adjust the room temperature. *"It is hot or cold,"* he shakes his head, *women*. He lay back down on the sofa and falls asleep.

Madi is awake well before Liam. She is careful not to wake him. It is his day off, too. He needs his rest. She tiptoes around the kitchen to find preparations for breakfast. She puts on the coffee.

Liam wakes to the perking sound of the coffee pot.

"Good morning, Madi," Liam speaks.

"I am sorry," Madi replies. "I did not mean to wake you."

"It is all right," he says.

"I need to get up anyway," Liam says. "The coffee smells great."

"Are you hungry?" Madi replies.

"I am going to fry some eggs and put some toast on."

"That sounds great," Liam replies. "Yes, please."

"I will set the table soon," she says.

"Is milk, ok?" Madi asks.

"Yes, milk is good," Liam says. "And a coffee please."

"It will be on the table in fifteen minutes," Madi says.

Madi and Liam finish their breakfast and have the day away from the diner.

"I need to be home by noon," Liam says. "I thought we could go for a walk, first."

"I would like that," Madi replies.

Madi and Liam prepare to go outdoors. They are off on Madi's regular trail. Madi knows Liam has something on his mind. The sun is bright. They had fresh snow last night. The road is packed with hard fresh snow this morning.

"What is on your mind?" Madi asks.

Liam likes Madi's directness, sometimes. "We should start thinking about wedding dates," Liam says.

"Is there a favorite season that you favor?" Liam asks the question this time.

"Spring or fall are beautiful times of the year," Madi replies.

That sounds good," Liam says. "I am thinking May or September."

"We will make plans, soon," Liam replies.

"We need a budget," Liam replies. "We will be paying for this from our savings."

"We will talk more over the weekend," Liam says.

"Sounds good," Madi replies.

Madi and Liam walk back to the house. Madi opens the front door.

Liam grabs his stuff, kisses her goodbye, and heads for home.

Madi has things to think about, too. It is all good. Madi already knows what she wants. She wants it quiet. She wants a small wedding, Spring, or Fall, it does not matter. She does prefer the green for pictures. These are the important things for Madi, happy memories. She wants the people at her wedding that matter most.

Madi already made her decision. Her dream is elopement. She is not sure Liam will approve. He has a part in this decision, too.

Madi enjoys the rest of her day. Tomorrow is back to the routine.

January is cold. Madi dresses up warm every day before she leaves for work. Madi and Liam hope to go skiing this month.

Madi and Liam join the family for Christmas at Doris' home. It is a beautiful evening. They laugh before and after dinner. The ladies help clear the table and clean the kitchen. The men disappear after dinner. They do what men do after a big dinner, maybe smoke their pipe or walk the dogs.

Madi and Liam sit down in the middle of January and decide on a wedding date. They decide on Saturday, the twenty-third of May this year. They like the idea of an elopement. The simplicity of it all and the cost factor is a great idea. Madi and Liam have prayed about it. They feel good about their decisions. They next step is to let the family know. They will do so, soon.

They want the particulars of the day in order, first. Both, Madi and Liam like their homeland. There are so many beautiful places to share the day together, in this country. They have places selected, and they will make their decision by the end of the month.

Twenty-Nine

The year is moving forward. Madi and Liam have final wedding plans. They decide to stay in Canada. Madi recommends her favorite resort. They have beautiful grounds. It has a lovely room with dining. They can stay for a night and enjoy the outdoors.

Liam books the resort. They let their family know of their decisions. They will each ask a close friend to stand up with them. The photographer is booked. They will take a week honeymoon, somewhere warm. They will work between the wedding day and the honeymoon in July.

Madi's birthday is approaching in the middle of April. Liam wants to do something nice for her. It is her twenty-fifth, this year. Madi has everything she needs. She is content. Liam wants to get away. He will find a new place they have not seen in the west, of course. The time of year indicates the Okanagan to be good. They will enjoy the water and the mountains, spend a couple of days hiking and dining out in various places. Liam books the room out of town. They will travel out the day before her birthday, on the eleventh, and drive home on the thirteenth. He keeps it a surprise.

It is going to be an eventful year full of excitement and love. Both, Madi and Liam enjoy their adventures. It is going to be a blessed year.

Liam goes back to his days' work.

Madi interrupts him. "Good morning," she says.

"Are you busy?" she asks.

"Good morning," Liam replies.

"I need some help out here," Madi says. "It is getting busy."

"I will be right there," Liam says.

They go about the business of the rest of the day. They say good night and go their separate ways. The next few weeks will be business as usual.

Madi's birthday is coming soon.

Madi notices Liam has her booked off the schedule over her birthday, and himself as well. She knows he has plans.

"Are we doing something on these, days?" she asks pointing to the schedule.

"Yes," he replies. "It is a surprise."

"Get yourself packed, we are heading out Monday, mid-morning to the Okanagan," Liam replies.

Madi is excited. She has only been to the Okanagan once when she was a little girl. She has memories that have long since faded. The country there she knows to be beautiful. The evergreens, the waters below the mountains, big game, new kinds of birds singing and fine dining. All the things she enjoys treating herself to, as she can afford. Now, to spend it with someone she loves.

Madi is packed, and Liam, too. She fuels her car. They decide to take her car.

They pack the car in the early morning.

Madi makes coffee in her travel mug. She grabs her purse and is on her way out the door.

Liam arrives. He locks his truck. He, too, has his coffee mug in his hand.

Liam drives. They are on the long road out of town. The radio playing softly in the background. They enjoy the sweetness of their conversation.

It is Madi who breaks the silence, first. "Liam what time do you expect to arrive today?" Madi asks.

"I estimate a couple of hours to arrive at the hotel," Liam replies.

"We will unpack and rest," Liam says. "We will drive around and find a lovely place to have dinner tomorrow, night."

"Thank you, Liam," Madi replies. "I am happy."

"I am happy, too, Madi," Liam says.

Liam drives in quietness. They stop along the way to stretch, grab a coffee, and take a washroom break.

Madi and Liam make their way back to the car. They are back on the road, again.

They arrive at the hotel after the noon hour. Liam parks the car. He checks into the hotel. He returns with the keys and hands them to Madi.

Madi has the bags unloaded outside of the car.

Liam parks the car. He locks the doors and joins Madi. Inside the hotel room they unpack their things.

Both, Madi and Liam decide they need a rest before heading out to explore the new town.

It is approaching dusk when they wake from their nap. They freshen up before heading out on the town. Madi and Liam agree it will be nice to sit and eat dinner at a nice table. Neither of them, are keen on take out. They drive a block or two, to the main street, at the recommendation of the hotel attendant. They find a diner and enjoy a hot sate noodle soup. It is a quiet dinner with little conversation. It has been a long drive.

Liam picks up a couple of bottles of ginger ale at Madi's request. Hotel rooms can be dry. It is a nice beverage any time of day. They arrive back at the hotel. They each have a quick shower and warm up in their night wear. They find their comfort zone and a decent movie. Madi sits close beside Liam's bed while he enjoys the action in the movie. It is a guy thing.

Madi endures.

Madi falls asleep.

Liam watches the movie right to the end. He does not want to disturb Madi, as she lay asleep across the bed. Liam moves to Madi's bed to rest. Liam is soon asleep, himself.

Madi rises early. She wakes up in Liam's bed. She blushes. Madi turns around and does not see Liam. She stands up and walks to the bathroom. She sees him sound asleep on her bed. Madi lets him sleep.

Madi takes the time to herself. She showers and dresses.

It is her birthday today, she smiles. She is twenty-five.

Liam wakes in the other room. He hears Madi coming and going in the other room. It is time for him to get up. He has overslept.

"Happy Birthday, Madi," he speaks.

"Thank you," Madi replies.

"Is the bathroom free," Liam replies.

"Yes," she says. "It is all yours."

"The coffee is on," she says.

"It is not the best coffee," Madi replies. "It will do."

"Sounds good," Liam replies.

"Give me fifteen minutes," he says. "I will be ready, soon."

"We will go for breakfast," he says.

Madi and Liam are back in the car. The same music playing softly. Liam is behind the wheel. Madi is trying to find directions on her telephone.

They find a truck stop and order their usual breakfast. They cannot wait for a good cup of coffee. At the least, it is not five dollars for each cup. They are grateful. Both, Madi and Liam work hard and try to be careful with their money and live within their means.

"Have you thought about what you would like for dinner?" he asks breaking the silence.

"Something simple," Madi replies. "Let's find a chicken place with a salad bar."

They finish breakfast. Liam pays the bill.

Madi rises to use the ladies room. They meet at the car. They are on their way to see the town. They want to find a museum or a heritage site open, today. They settle on a nice park to walk around the water. The ice has melted, and the water is dirty. The fountain is off. It is not the most beautiful time of year in the town. The fresh air is nice. They find a bike path. There are people coming and going with their dogs and children walking along the path.

The walk together until the noon hour. Liam is ready to head back, and Madi, too. They take their drive around the town. They stop by a shopping plaza and have a look around. They pass a little café and check it out. It is a lovely place. They have a bite to eat. They walk around the plaza for an hour.

Madi is ready to go back to the hotel. She wants to rest.

The next morning, they will be heading home. It will be back to their routine.

Their thoughts will be on Madi's moving out. The wedding plans will be next. Madi set the thoughts aside. One thing at a time.

Madi and Liam head back to the hotel. They grab a coffee refill on the way home.

"Do we still have water at the room?" Liam asks.

"Yes," Madi replies, "two or three bottles."

"I will get more in the morning before we head out," Liam says handing Madi her coffee.

"Thank you," Madi says.

They arrive at the hotel. They sit down on the bed. Liam grabs the remote and surfs the TV channels. There must be something to watch this afternoon.

"Yes, maybe not," Madi replies. "I do not watch much TV."

"I prefer to read," she says.

"I watch a little TV, Madi," Liam says.

"It is mostly noise in the background," Liam replies. "It helps me to unwind at the end of the day."

Liam finds an old western playing and parks the TV. It plays while they talk and finish their coffee.

They fall asleep.

Madi wakes in a half hour, and Liam shortly, thereafter.

Liam decides an early dinner will be good.

They will retire early. It will be nice to be on the road at a decent hour.

Madi agrees.

They tidy up and head down to the café for dinner.

They enjoy a lovely dinner. Liam hands her a small box after dinner.

"Happy Birthday, again," Liam replies.

"Thank you, Liam," Madi opens the box. She finds a beautiful gold pendant with a diamond encased in the center; love Liam neatly engraved in the back.

"It is beautiful," Madi smiles.

"I love you," she says.

"I love you, too," Liam says. "I am trying to show my love to you."

"It is about giving," Liam says.

"We are still in good years." Liam speaks.

"There will be lean years," Liam says, "when I cannot do these things."

"I will look after them," Madi replies. "I know you love me."

"I will always love you and provide for you to the best of my ability," Liam speaks. "I just ask you to be the helpmate I need you to be."

"I want to be the person I am today, the rest of my days," Madi says.

Back at the room, Madi and Liam are tidying up to prepare for the morning. They watch a movie, falling asleep next to one another.

Madi slept for an hour.

Madi wakes and finds her way to her own bed.

Madi is soon back to sleep.

Thirty

Madi and Liam wake up early. They are back in the car with fresh coffee, and water. They are on the road. They is a lot to do when they arrive home.

Liam pulls into Madi's driveway. It is Wednesday morning. He walks through the front door behind her.

Madi drops her bags inside and turns around to see Liam.

"Are you going to stay for a bit?" she asks.

"I should get home," Liam replies. "I need to go into the diner, later."

"We are both on the schedule, tomorrow, get some rest," Liam replies. He whispers something in her ear and kisses her good-bye.

She smiles back and returns the gesture. "See you tomorrow," she replies.

Liam leaves out her front door.

Madi looks around her house. She has boxes piled high in her storage. She has packing to do. Her lease expires this month. She will be moving into Liam's house, soon. It is only weeks before their wedding day. Liam offered her the second bedroom on the upper level. It is across the hall from his room.

Liam has promised to help her downsize and purge her extra furniture.

Madi makes her wish list of things she wishes to keep. She unpacks her bags. Madi jumps in the shower to wipe away her travel tiredness.

Madi enjoys a cup of coffee and sits down with her book. She does not have a dull moment in her life. Her mother has left a birthday message on her telephone. She reaches for her telephone. She dials her mother's number.

Elisabeth picks up the telephone.

"Hello," mom says.

"Hello, mom," Madi says. "Thank you for the birthday wish."

"You are welcome," mom replies.

"Did you do anything interesting?" mom asks.

Madi does not share the details. "I went out of town," Madi replies. "A little getaway."

"I hope you had a good rest," mom replies.

"I did very much," Madi says. "It was pleasant."

"I am back to the routine, tomorrow," Madi says. "I have lots to do in the next couple of weeks."

Madi and Liam need to talk on Sunday. It is time to get down to real life.

Liam follows Madi home Sunday evening after work. They bring leftovers home from the diner for dinner, that night. They share a dinner together at Madi's dinner table.

"We have a lot of work to do in the next couple of weeks," Liam speaks, first.

"Yes," Madi replies.

"We need to get organized," he replies.

"We need to finalize the wedding plans, this week," Liam says.

"Yes," Madi replies.

"You are home on Monday?" Liam asks. "Let's sit down tomorrow night and make these decisions."

Madi smiles. She is ready to move forward into her new life.

Liam looks around her two-bedroom apartment size townhome. "The next step is to get your things over to the house," he says.

"Decide what you will keep," Liam says. "I will help you next week with the move."

Liam follows Madi to the front room with his tea. They sit together on the sofa. They enjoy conversation before Liam needs to head home. Liam works tomorrow. They have a busy couple of weeks ahead, physical, and emotional. They need their rest.

Madi kisses Liam goodnight at the front door.

Liam heads home.

Madi is in bed early.

She wakes up on a regular day, Monday morning. She enjoys a coffee and her breakfast. Madi makes plans for dinner for Liam and herself, tonight.

Madi calls Liam mid-Morning, to let him know of the dinner plans. He thanks her and indicates to arrive around seven o'clock.

It is a beautiful day. Madi puts her coat and shoes on and heads outside for a walk. She enjoys her usual path. She waves at Ron. He is outside pruning in his yard. Ron waves back and smiles. Madi looks forward to time to herself. It is a lovely morning, the birds are singing, the rabbits scurry under her feet. The rabbits love it when she stops to talk to them. She will never give up this part of her life. It is her time alone with God. It gives her strength each day. It is her time to recollect her thoughts and begin again. All her fears seem to fade when she gets alone in these quiet moments. The routine of the day seems to disappear.

Madi heads back to the house, stopping to talk with Ron on the last leg of her walk.

Madi shares with Ron, briefly. She does not talk of her private life. Her life is between her and Liam, now. Ron understands. She mentions Liam and her birthday getaway.

Ron wishes her a belated happy birthday.

Madi mentions she will be moving out at the end of this month. She will not be renewing her lease. Ron and Brenda knew this day would come. They are happy for her. Her life is heading in the right direction.

Madi says goodbye and mentions Liam will be arriving later, today.

Liam arrives promptly at seven o'clock at Madi's door.

Madi prepares a simple dinner. She takes the chicken breasts from the oven. She sets a large garden salad on the table. The rice is in the steamer and will finish in the next ten minutes. The table is set.

Liam sits himself at the dinner table. He is comfortable in her home, now.

"Dinner looks great," he says.

"Thank you," Madi smiles.

Madi sets the chicken on the table. She places the rice on the table.

Madi sits down at the table. She asks Liam to say the blessing.

Liam reaches over and takes Madi's hand. They bow their heads and ask for God's blessing on the food, and the week.

Liam helps Madi clear the table.

Madi puts the leftover food in the fridge.

Madi and Liam retire to the front room with a pen and paper.

Liam mentions he wants to get the wedding plans done tonight. "Do you really want to elope, Madi?" Liam asks.

"It is probably not the best idea," Madi replies, "as simple as it seems."

Liam agrees.

The timing is not right for the planned date. "I am sure we can still book a hall and a place to eat," Liam replies.

"Are you game to stay in town?" he asks. Madi and Liam had already agreed the resort was not right. Liam confirmed the cancellations were complete.

"I am fine with staying in town," Madi says. "I do not want a large group."

"Immediate family, and Ron and Brenda are enough from my side," Madi says, "and your list."

"That sounds good to me," Liam replies. "We can cap the group at fifteen."

Madi agrees, she smiles at Liam. "Let's book the hall, near mom and dads," Madi says. "There is a beautiful green space with trees."

"That sounds perfect," Liam says.

"I can make arrangements, tomorrow," Madi says. "I will put a deposit on my credit card."

"Keep me posted with what you spend," Liam says. "I will cover it."

"I will put together invitations at the office," Madi replies. "I will need invitees names and addresses."

"The invitations need to get out by the end of this week." she says.

"Sounds good," Liam replies. "We can call your parents tomorrow evening."

"I am thinking," Liam says. "We may bring a caterer to the diner."

"That is a clever idea," Madi replies. "Salads and pasta are fine with me."

"Chicken parmigiana, spaghetti, meatballs with sauce, my thoughts," Madi replies. "I will let you manage it."

"It is only fifteen of us," Liam says. "We are small enough it can be served rather than buffet."

"I will put a menu together," Liam replies. "And hire the kitchen staff for the night."

"We are almost done," Liam says.

"I have a decent suit and the rings," Liam replies. "You need a gown."

"It is done," Madi replies. "It will be ready in time."

"It sounds like we are under control," Liam says. "Let's get it done."

"Let's get the move done this weekend," Liam speaks to Madi.

Madi's thoughts are back on the move. She is not looking forward to it. She has collected so many things over the few years in her home. She has been here forever. Madi has so much to do with purging.

Madi will have to sell what she can, and the rest will go to the consignment store.

Liam likes how Madi manages her home. It is with skill and yet a gift.

Liam looks at his watch. It is getting late. Liam works on Tuesday.

Madi is off, again tomorrow.

Madi walks Liam to the front door. Liam kisses her goodnight.

Madi hears his truck start and then he is gone.

Madi is glad to have some time to herself before bed. She catches herself yawning.

Madi is asleep in her bed not to long after Liam departs.

Thirty-One

The next couple of weeks are busy for both Madi and Liam. The wedding day plans are in place for Saturday, the twenty-third of May. Madi's gown is on order and the catering is in place.

Madi and Liam have completed the invitations and delivered them, respectively. Of course, mom and dads will be hand delivered in person. Ron and Brenda are excited, they are happy for both, Madi and Liam. Madi and Liam do deserve each other. They both work hard. They share and love the outdoors. They share and grow together every day.

Madi spends her days off, first she organizes Liam's place. She will store stuff in his garage. She makes room in what is to be her bedroom for now. It will all be temporary, of course.

Madi takes a week to go through all her belongings. Her kitchen stuff is all a keeper including her dining room table. Her front room furniture is set aside to sell. It will go to the garage. The bedroom set will go to Madi's temporary room. The bathroom, clothes, and linens and sundry will all transport to the new home.

Liam stops by every evening to help her. He booked the truck early enough to give Brenda and Madi enough time to clean the place before handing in the key.

The place is vacant and clean. The end of the month is near.

Madi smiles as she walks out the front door. She stands and looks at the front veranda. She has so many memories in this place. It will soon all be behind her. She is beginning, again. A new life. An old friend.

Madi knows there will be good times and tough times. She is ready to embrace her future.

Ron and Brenda walk across the road and stand beside her.

"We will miss you, Madi," Ron says giving her a hug.

Brenda hugs Madi.

Madi wipes away her tears. It is a good move. She is trying hard to keep her composure. She will soon be a married woman.

Madi drives to Liam's not looking back. She smiles and sings softly with the radio.

Madi walks inside Liam's home. He had keys made for her the other night.

"Home Sweet Home," she says as she checks out each room. Madi will need to find her comfort zone.

Madi hears Liam pull up into the driveway. He walks through the front room door. Madi is happy to see him. He kisses her on the cheek and hangs up his coat. He puts his shoes on the mat. He makes his exit upstairs.

Liam comes back downstairs.

"You are in a rush," Madi says.

"There is plenty on my mind, dear," Liam says. "It is all good."

"Welcome home," Liam replies. "Please make yourself at home."

"Thank you," Madi says. "I will."

Madi has no reservations with Liam. She says it like it is.

Liam is the same.

Madi and Liam need to sit down and discuss the household chores.

Madi is comfortable the kitchen is hers. She rummages through the pantry, fridge, and freezer to plan dinner. They agree to begin eating dinners together at home. They will share breakfast and midday dinner at the diner. Madi will manage the regular cleaning and maintenance duties.

Of course, she is comfortable to say the garage, including the vehicles, are Liam's duties. They will share the lawn and garden duties.

Madi feels it is fair. Madi works hard at the diner. She does carry the lighter load there. The way Liam wants it. He wants her more in the home and to have a life there, too.

They are only weeks from the wedding. Everything is all in place.

Her friends tell her the stress is in the day. Madi has that to look forward to.

Madi's dress is in. It fits perfect. She has it tucked away in the closet. Madi keeps it hidden from Liam. She still needs to find shoes. She is looking for a simple, color matched slip-on shoe. Madi likes comfort.

Madi and Liam get through the next week business as usual. The wedding day plans are in place. They travel to work together the days they can.

Liam takes his days off when he can. On those days, Madi drives herself to the diner.

Friends warn them of spending too much time together. They are both focused. Madi and Liam see each other at the end of the day, like most working couples. At work, they are too busy for most idle conversation.

Madi settles herself into her own bedroom. It is full. Her bed is there. Her clothes are hanging in the closet. Her dainties are all around her.

Madi is happy.

Thirty-Two

Madi and Liam wake early the morning of their wedding. The diner is prepared and closed for the day. Their customers are aware of Madi and Liam's day. Congratulation cards and gifts keep arriving at the diner. They receive each card and gift with gratitude.

The kitchen staff will check into the diner early afternoon to begin dinner preparations. They will pick up the keys in the morning. Liam has managed it all.

Madi is preparing herself. She is perspiring and nervous. She did not expect this. She wipes herself dry after her shower. She puts on a pair of cotton slacks and a cotton dress shirt.

Madi fusses over her hair. Brenda and her mother come by to help her get into her gown. Her parents drive her to the hall.

Liam is already there. He is coordinating it all. He likes to be the boss. He is good at it. People like Liam.

You can call it charisma; others call it nice. Madi calls it friendly.

Madi does her best to keep herself hidden. She sees the minister. He directs Liam into the hall. It is time to get the ceremony going.

Madi has the hall done up simple. She has organized it with the help of Brenda and her mother, late last night.

It is a simple ceremony. It is about an hour long. Madi walks the aisle with her father. He gives her away to Liam. They both smile.

Madi looks at Liam.

Liam looks at Madi. "You look beautiful," he whispers.

"Thank you," Madi replies with a smile.

Madi saves her words for later. The minister is about to speak.

They are both thankful. No one is present to contest the wedding. That means each person in the room is in support of their decision. Madi and Liam, both smile at one another again.

The minister turns to each of them. "Are you ready?" he asks.

Madi and Liam both nod the affirmative.

The minister continues, he marries them in the little room, as they have planned. Their lives will never be the same. Two people become one under their God, by their choice.

They arrive at the diner in time for dinner. It is casual. They are all family and close friends. Each group seats themselves where they are most comfortable. Everyone knows the diner. Madi's parents do not care for the place. They do not get out much. They are seeming to endure. The caterers bring ice water to the tables. They serve coffee and tea. They serve the salad, and the meal soon, thereafter. Dessert is set out on the buffet table. They have various square on plates.

Madi and Liam have built their own tradition of simplicity with success.

The meal is lovely. Madi and Liam are happy with their day. There are toasts made to their future and happiness. They open gifts and cards, over dessert.

The day finishes well. Well, done!

111

It is not long, and they are saying goodbye. The happy couple are soon in their truck heading home. They are exhausted. They will be up early in the morning to do the clean up.

Tonight, is there first night to be together. Madi is scared. She embraces her future with Liam. She knows he is the man she has chosen to be with.

The rest of the night is beautiful. Madi falls asleep much later in Liam arms. Neither of them stir all night.

Thirty-Three

Madi wakes up first, Sunday morning. The sun is shining. She is a little uncomfortable. For a moment she feels she is at her old place. Madi feels Liam next to her. She feels different. They are now beyond the place of friendship. Madi is Liam's wife. She has put her trust in this man's love. It is a bit overwhelming. She will have to embrace it. Sleeping in her own bed gave her a sense of control of her own life. It will all be different, now.

Madi and Liam will pray everyday, together.

Madi heads down the stairs and puts the coffee on and prepares breakfast. They need to clean up the hall, today. Madi will hand in the keys on Monday.

Madi and Liam will take their honeymoon in the summer. These plans are tentative. It will happen in early August in their slower time at the diner.

Madi has breakfast ready. She hears Liam rising.

"Breakfast is ready," she calls to Liam.

"I will be there soon," Liam replies.

Liam comes down the stairs. He realizes it is the first day of their married life. He looks at his wife and smiles.

"We made it," Liam says.

"How does it feel to be my wife?" he asks.

"I am adjusting," Madi says with a smile.

Liam does not understand. He appreciates her honesty. He smiles and kisses her on the lips. There is passion between them, again. They are in love.

Madi serves his breakfast. "We need to get the hall cleaned up, soon," Madi says.

"This afternoon we can enjoy each other," Madi says to Liam with a smile.

Liam likes Madi's honesty and eager to please.

They finish breakfast and drive over to the hall. They want to get it done. They have other things to do, today.

Madi and Liam arrive at the hall. They look around and split the duties. Decorations come down and are put into bags. The kitchen is tidy. They put the chairs away. They sweep and wash the floor. The two of them wrap it up in a couple of hours. They will soon be home.

Madi and Liam arrive home. They are not hungry. They have a glass of water.

Liam picks Madi off the floor and carries her upstairs to their bedroom.

Madi giggles. She is too heavy for this. She lets Liam have his fun.

"This is not funny, Liam Nam," Madi replies.

Liam laughs.

Madi laughs.

They enjoy each other for a time and fall asleep in each others' arms.

Liam is back to work, tomorrow.

Madi will tend to the house. She still has things to do. It dreadfully needs a woman's touch for Madi to be comfortable. She is thankful Liam has given her the liberty to do so. They do not easily offend each other.

Madi still has her extra paperwork to do including all her legal name changes. They decide to keep separate banking and share as they require. There is nothing hidden between Madi and Liam.

Liam has plans to put Madi's name on the title of the house. He wants to bring her into the business. He has nothing to keep from Madi. He loves and trusts her. It is about looking after each other. They want the other to be able to manage their life.

The stuff you never want to think about, but you need to. Liam's faith is growing every day.

Madi and Liam are careful to take time every day to pray together and share God's word.

Madi has learned to be wise who to let in her home. Her home is a quiet place. She does not let strangers into her home. She has a handful of friends and even they meet outside of their homes for coffee or for lunch. Madi and Liam work hard. Their home is their refuge.

Madi learns the virtue of marriage from reading her Bible. It is a sacred union between a man and a woman.

Madi is not ready to go back to church. Now, being married she is even more reserved to protect their privacy.

Madi and Liam will need to discuss it and pray about it. They will trust God to lead them to the right place in time.

Thirty-Four

Madi is back to work and business as usual, Wednesday morning. Liam is home for the next couple of days. Madi will drive herself to work. It is her turn to hold down the diner. She arrives at work early to open the place. She unlocks the doors, checks the washrooms, walks around each of the tables, tidying as she goes along.

Doris drives up, shortly after Madi.

Doris greets Madi with a smile.

"Good morning, Doris," Madi says with a smile.

Doris is always pleasant to work with. Madi knows her well enough. Doris runs a strong house. Her and her husband, both do. Her husband is old school and lets Doris manage the load. He provides well for his house.

Madi and Liam manage their home a little different. It is their choice. Madi relies on Liam to share the home duties. Liam relies on Madi to share the work duties. Together they are better.

They both know they have difficult years ahead. Madi is thankful Liam has a good understanding of economics. It comes with running his own business. Liam understands the trends and the impacts of business. There are times when none of it makes sense. They need to trust in God. It is a walk of faith with wisdom.

Madi goes back to the tasks of the day. The customers are arriving. Doris is ready in the kitchen.

Madi begins seating her first customers as they come through the door. She is smiling. Madi places orders one at a time, filling coffee mugs. It is not long before the diner is full of customers.

Doris' frying pans are steady with frying bacon and eggs.

Madi picks up orders as the plates come ready and takes them to their tables.

The breakfast shift comes and goes, lunch guests will arrive, soon.

Madi will be happy to see Becky arrive.

Liam has put Becky on the dinner shift. She has a good handle on the processes, now. The customers like her.

Madi is so glad to have her afternoons.

Becky arrives on time.

"Good afternoon, Becky," Madi says. Madi is happy to see her.

"Good afternoon, Madi," Becky replies.

"I am mostly, cleaned up," Madi replies. "Grab a coffee and relax."

"I will be heading home, soon," Madi replies.

"Thank you," Becky says. "I will do that."

Madi leaves the diner. She cannot wait to get home. Madi makes a wrong turn toward the old house. She chuckles. She too is a creature of habit of old days. It takes time to transition to new things. Madi corrects herself. She continues down the road to Liam's home.

It is now, Madi and Liam's home. Madi adds her elegant touch to the once masculine décor of the home.

Madi is careful to let Liam in on any major changes she thinks may fit. The interior paint is due, but it can wait. She focuses on the pretties.

Madi arrives at the front door.

Liam is sitting on the front veranda with a glass of water. His recent health scare taught him to pace himself.

Madi joins him. She grabs herself a glass of ice water and sits next to him. Madi engages in conversation about her day.

"How was your day?" Liam asks.

"It was busy," Madi replies sipping her water. "I was happy to see Becky."

"I am glad to be home," Madi says.

"How was your day? Madi asks.

"It was good," Liam replies.

"I missed you," he continues. "I did get a few things done around the house."

"I took hamburger out of the freezer for dinner," Liam replies.

"Do you have plans for dinner?" Madi asks.

"I am thinking spaghetti," Liam replies.

"I can manage dinner," he says. "Take some time for yourself."

Madi laughs.

Madi and Liam always have stuff to do.

"Thank you," Madi says. "I will let you manage dinner."

"I can find stuff to do," she replies.

Liam looks up at Madi, "I added your name to the title of the house, today."

Madi looks at Liam, "Ok," Madi speaks.

"I have had plans to sell," Liam replies. "It is now both of our decision."

"I have plans to bring you into the business," Liam says. "It is a little more complex."

"It will happen in time," Liam continues.

"I will leave most of the financial decisions to you, Liam," Madi replies. "I am quite comfortable for now."

"It is more than we need," Madi says. "We can still purge some."

"I do agree with you," Liam says. "We can deal with that in the late fall."

"I still want to take you a on a honeymoon," Liam speaks.

"We talked about August," Madi replies, "close to home, please."

"I am happy to take the holiday trailer," Madi says, "and explore the western provinces."

Liam looks at Madi, "that sounds like a good idea," he replies.

"We will make plans in the next few weeks," Liam replies. "The shifts at the diner need to be covered, first."

Thirty-Five

Madi and Liam retire early for the evening.

Liam's spaghetti was lovely to come home to after a long day. Madi did not have to cook or clean up. A pleasant moment of her day.

Madi is thankful Liam enjoys doing the things he needs to do everyday.

They talk into the evening for a little awhile. Madi fell asleep in his arms.

Liam is not far behind her.

Madi wakes to the sun coming through the window.

Liam is already up with the coffee pot on. He is having his first cup of coffee.

Madi is in the shower. She dresses quickly. She wants to share a coffee with Liam before heading to work.

"Good morning," Madi says.

Liam hears her coming down the stairs. He has a fresh cup of coffee on the table waiting for her.

"Thank you," Madi says. "I do not have much time."

"We cannot do this every day," Liam replies. "Enjoy it when we can."

Madi sits down. She sips her coffee. "*It is great to enjoy a coffee first thing in the morning with someone that loves you,* "she thinks to herself.

Madi looks at her watch. "I best be going," she kisses Liam goodbye.

Liam returns the kiss. "Goodbye, enjoy your day."

Madi looks at him and smiles. "I will."

Madi walks out the door closing it softly behind her. She is in her car and on the way to the diner. She is running five minutes late. This is unusual for Madi. It is all good. It will work out all right.

Madi arrives at the diner. It is business as usual, all day. Madi tends to her regulars at breakfast and lunch.

Becky arrives on time for her dinner shift.

Madi completes her closing functions and hangs up her apron. She says her goodbyes and heads home.

Madi arrives home to find Liam on the veranda. She joins him with a glass of ice water.

Liam smiles at her.

"It is another good day," Madi says, "business as usual."

"I am glad to be home," she says.

"I am happy you are home," Liam says.

"I did not get anything out for dinner," Liam replies. "It is leftovers or we go out."

"Let's go out," Madi says.

"I am good with that," Liam replies. "Our favorite diner across town will be fun."

"I like that idea. "Madi replies.

Madi jumps in the shower and freshens up.

They arrive at the diner after the dinner rush. There are two couples seated inside. They walk through the front door. The server finds them a small table in the corner. It is a great place for a quiet date off the rush hour. The food is great, and the comrade is great.

Liam frequents the place. He enjoys taking Madi here. He knows the owner. They share business ideas.

Madi is learning. She is getting to know more about Liam every day. She is learning who his friends are. His friends are businesspeople.

Liam knows his friendships will change. He is married, now. He is changing the way he thinks about Madi as well as himself. Liam is becoming home and family oriented.

Madi does not have close friends other than Liam. Liam is her best friend. Madi makes friends and they come and go. Madi, too remains home focused, first, and finds herself becoming family focused.

Madi and Liam finish their dinner.

Liam drives home.

It is getting late. They are working in the morning. They retire early and fall asleep, very soon.

They wake up with the sun pouring through their bedroom window.

Liam jumps in the shower, first. Madi, second, behind him.

Liam will drive them both into work.

They have their coffee and breakfast at the diner.

Liam is anxious to get into work and catch up after his days off.

Madi is feeling a little sick this morning. She does not feel like the coffee. She brushes the feelings aside and focuses on her duties.

It is a longer day than normal. The sick feeling comes and goes.

Madi feels fine as soon as she arrives home. She is vibrant.

Madi prepares dinner.

Madi and Liam talk through dinner.

Madi's next day feels the same. The feeling hits her the same each morning.

Madi goes through her days. She has days better than others. Madi's intuition is strong. She still makes no mention of it to Liam.

Sunday night comes around. Madi and Liam are sitting on the veranda watching the sun set.

Madi turns to Liam. "I should have said something sooner," she speaks.

Liam turns to Madi. "Say what?" Liam asks.

"I have been feeling ill," Madi says, "most morning through the week."

"Are you pregnant?" Liam says with a smile.

"I think so," Madi smiles.

"I have an appointment to see the doctor, tomorrow," Madi says.

"This is not a problem," Liam says. "You need your rest."

Madi does need to relax and rest.

Liam cautions her to take care of herself first. Her workload will lessen as she moves further along. He will make sure of that.

Liam is happy.

Madi is happy.

They promise to work through these days together. The honeymoon becomes a faded memory. They have more important things to focus on.

Madi and Liam agree to stay close to home and remain private through this time.

Liam is most concerned with keeping Madi and baby comfortable and safe.

Madi's doctor prepares her with what to expect.

Liam finds himself praying often for both Madi and the baby's safety.

Liam books himself and Madi off work for a couple of weeks in July. He decides they will stay home and share the days together. They may venture out on a day trip, or overnight, together.

Their little family will soon be complete.

Madi and Liam smile.

Thirty-Six

The month of July comes in with heavy rains for the first week. It quickly turns to the typical heat of the season. It is not long before the ground is dry and cracking. Liam is glad he does not farm. Farming as he sees it, is either rich or poor and depends on the climate, rain, or sun. Liam wants a little more certainty for his future and his growing family.

The diner is not perfect, but it brings in a steady income. It is demanding work but at least it will feed his family. Liam is happy to have a wife as Madi to stand beside him for all these years. There are days he shakes his head at all the blessings in his life. His home is tidy, and the grounds are neat. The diner is the same. They have time to enjoy life together outside of their workload.

It is still early to get excited about the growing baby. Madi is a few weeks along in her pregnancy. They both decide to keep it a secret. They see people come and go all day and enjoy their quiet time at home.

Madi joins Liam on the front step.

Madi is carrying two lemonades. Liam stands up and takes his glass from her.

"Thank you, Liam," Madi says.

"You are welcome," he replies. "We may have to get are hats on."

"The sun is blistering hot," he replies.

"I feel it," Madi replies. "I can get you one."

"It is ok," Liam replies. "I will get up if I need to."

Madi has been drinking lemon water all day.

Liam has a bad habit of not drinking enough fluid.

Madi is constantly on his case about it. She does not need him getting heat stroke.

Madi will purchase a water cooler for him. He hates tap water. The filtered water jugs are not big enough to keep them both in enough water.

"It looks like we will be walking in the cool of the evenings," Madi says.

"That is a good idea," Liam replies.

"I would like to take you to the beach." Liam says. "If the heat will slow down for a day or two."

"We have the air conditioner, Liam," Madi says. "I do not need to go anywhere."

Madi and Liam are eating light meals. They do not want to eat at all.

Madi and Liam watch movies until the late evening.

Liam can feel the temperature dropping. "I think it may be cool enough to get some sleep," Liam says.

"Yes, I hope you are right," Madi says. "I am ready to sleep."

"Let's go," Liam says. "He takes her hand and leads her up the stairs."

Madi undresses and slips her gown over her head and crawls into bed first.

Liam is close behind her. He turns out the lights and crawls under the top sheet beside her.

Madi is asleep long before Liam.

Liam tosses, turns, and falls asleep a little later.

Madi wakes the next morning her bright sunny self. Liam is still asleep. She lets him sleep. She skips the shower. She does not want to wake him.

Madi turns the coffee pot on. She retires to the front room. She picks up her Bible from the side table and opens the page where she left off the other morning. Madi is reading in the book of Psalms. She started with the first Psalm. She is reading near the twenty-second Psalm, now. She continues into the next couple of chapters.

She knows it is going to be another hot, muggy day. The sun is bright and hot already at eight o'clock in the morning. Madi fixes herself a cup of coffee the way she likes it. She sits at the kitchen table alone sipping a bit at a time. She does not hear Liam come up behind her. He leans over her right shoulder and kisses her on the cheek.

"Good morning, darling," Liam says.

Madi blushes. She is still a little shy with all this attention.

"Good morning, Liam," she replies with a smile.

"Are you feeling well?" Liam asks.

"I am doing good at the moment," she says smiling, kissing him gently on the cheek.

"Would you like a coffee? she asks.

"Yes, please," he replies.

Madi gets out of her seat and walks to the kitchen. She finds Liam's mug. She makes him his coffee as he likes it. She sets it on the table in front of him.

"What would you like for breakfast? she asks.

"I am hungry," Liam replies, "eggs and toast, please."

"Me, too," Madi pulls her pans out and prepares them both breakfast. She takes his plate to the table. She smiles.

Madi sits down next to Liam with her breakfast in front of her.

"Thank you," Liam says.

"It looks great," Liam says the blessing. They both eat, hungrily.

"It looks like we are staying around the house, today," Liam says. "We are in for another hot one."

Madi clears the table putting the plates and mugs in the sink.

"I am heading up to shower," Madi says.

"Save me some hot water," Liam replies.

Madi smiles back at him. "We may want the cool water this afternoon," she replies.

"This is the truth," Liam replies.

It is not long before they are sitting on the front veranda drinking lemonade. Madi has her pitcher of lemonade with ice, this time. She knows they are going to need a refill or two of it today. Liam has his hat on. Madi does, too. Here they are sitting outside laughing and giggling like school kids, drinking lemonade in the heat of July. They are afraid to leave the house on their days off. There is nowhere to go in Nucton except the mall. The last place they want to go on their holiday.

They may as well make the best of it. Liam checks the weather forecast. It is looking good. It is supposed to rain the day after tomorrow. They only hope and pray.

The day passes by as normal.

Both Madi and Liam manage their best through the heat. They try and sleep in the cool of the afternoon. The blinds closed. The air conditioner is running most days. They are up late and eating late in cool temperature.

The next day the same. The grey skies come in around three o'clock in the afternoon. They think they may get out and do something.

"Do we dare head out for a bite to eat this evening," Liam says.

"I would like to get out of the house, Liam," Madi says.

"Let's do it," he replies. "Go get ready."

Madi runs up the stairs.

123

Liam is right behind her.

They both arrive at the front door in cool garments. Madi and Liam get their rain parkas. They are soon out the door. They can feel the cool breeze. Liam helps Madi into the truck. He gets into the driver's side.

They are off in Liam's truck.

Liam drives the distance to the other diner. The place is near full. The server manages to squeeze them into a corner table. They order their usual.

Madi has tea, and Liam orders a soft drink. The place is full of chatter. The community of people are happy to be out, too.

Madi and Liam join in the laughter around them.

Dinner is done. It is time to head home for the evening. The cool breeze surrounds them in the outside air.

"I would like to go for a walk, tonight," Madi says.

"A short one will be nice," Liam says.

Madi and Liam arrive at the house.

He parks the truck. He steps around to help Madi out of the truck. He locks the truck and puts his keys in his pocket. Liam takes Madi's hand, and they walk toward the pathway. They are talking about everything that comes into Madi's mind. Madi is talking about the baby and baby stuff.

Liam is trying to calm her anxiety. He tries to rein her into reality. She is becoming a chatter box. Liam is hoping she can continue to work. They need the money. He knows changes are coming. He is feeling new life about to happen for them.

Thirty-Seven

The summer passes by and Madi is feeling very pregnant. The symptoms are less frequent now. She manages to keep up with her shifts at work. She sleeps more at home.

Liam is carrying more of the load on the home front. It is putting more pressure on him. They manage but it is taking its toll on their relationship. Liam is finding himself leaving the house more all the time.

Madi feels something missing between them. It is not how she hoped their first year of marriage would happen. Her doctor gave her everything she needed to prepare.

Madi prays

Heavenly Father

Please bring Liam and I closer together in this time.
Help us to see the finish line.
Give us strength to endure and see your plan.

Amen

Madi can hear Liam come in the door. The front door closes behind him. He hangs his coat in the closet. His shoes fall against wall. He walks into the kitchen.

"Good afternoon," he says.

"How are you feeling?" he asks.

"I am ok," Madi says. "I am putting dinner together."

"Thank you," Liam says. "I am hungry." He kisses her on the cheek.

"The diner was busy today," Liam says.

"You need to talk to me," Liam continues.

"Let me know what you can manage," he says. "I need you strong at home more than the diner."

"I will let you know," Madi says.

"I mean it, Madi," Liam speaks. "Finances will be tight with you home."

"We will manage," Liam says. "You need your rest now."

"Yes, I know," Madi replies.

"Dinner is ready," Madi replies. "Help yourself." She bursts into tears and heads upstairs to the bedroom.

Madi wants to be alone.

Liam turns the oven off. He sets the dinner aside. He is not hungry, yet.

Liam knows this is all normal. He heads up the stairs after Madi. He finds her laying on the bed, sobbing. He lays beside her and holds her.

"Madi this is normal," he says. "We are going to have to learn to cope with it."

"I want to work through it all, Liam," Madi says.

"You do what you can," Liam replies.

"Maybe a couple of days each week," Liam speaks. "It will get you out of the house."

"I can do that, Liam," Madi replies. "The exercise will do me good."

"Let's go eat," Liam says. "It is getting cold."

"Dinner looks lovely," Liam says smiling at Madi.

"Thank you," Madi replies.

"If I am home," Madi says. "It is the least, I can do."

"Thank you," Liam says. "I appreciate it."

Madi smiles. She walks down the stairs with Liam behind her.

Liam sets the table.

Madi checks the dinner. She serves their plates placing Liam's in the microwave, first. She heats hers next. She joins Liam at the table.

Liam waits for her to join him. He blesses the food giving thanks to God.

The September month is still warm. It is cooling most every night. Madi and Liam go for a walk after dinner. The dishes are in the sink. Madi will do them in the morning.

Madi and Liam have prepared themselves for the next few months until the baby arrives. It will be instant in season and out of season.

Christmas time will be a quiet one together just the two of them. It will not be a traditional turkey for their first. They will be going out somewhere and enjoying others cooking.

Christmas day arrives.

Madi and Liam spend their morning doing Christmas stuff. It is a simple gift exchange. A small breakfast with coffee. Liam will find a place open if their favorite diner is not.

Madi and Liam share dinner together at their usual diner. Madi is showing a little. People start to notice her. Madi is not one to draw attention to herself.

Madi tries to show gratitude. She wants to be polite.

"I think I am done," Liam speaks.

"Are you ready to go, hon?" Liam asks.

"I think so," Madi replies. "Maybe a short walk."

"I think it is a good idea," he smiles.

Madi walks behind him on the way out of the diner. Liam helps her into the truck.

"Merry Christmas, Madi, I love you," Liam says kissing her gently on the lips.

"It is not always going to be as this," he speaks encouragingly.

"Merry Christmas, Liam," Madi replies. "I love you, too."

Liam longs for closeness with Madi. It has been a long time. He puts his thoughts aside. He parks the truck in their driveway and helps Madi out of the truck.

Madi puts her purse inside the door of the house. They put on warm gloves. He locks the front door behind them.

Liam puts Madi's hand in his. They go for a walk.

Liam walks them out into the moonlit sky. He wants to see the stars. They sit on a nearby park bench to get a full view of the open sky. The stars are sparkling and dancing throughout the sky. It is how God put each of them there.

Liam kisses Madi on the lips. He caresses her swollen body hoping to bring her comfort. Madi smiles. She reaches to him and kisses him softly on the mouth.

"It is one day at a time, my love," Liam says. "I will walk it with you."

"Thank you," Madi replies.

Liam takes her hand. They walk back to the house.

Thirty-Eight

The morning came early on February twenty-second. It is cold. The snow is hard packed. It is time. Madi knows it and Liam, too. Madi is wet with perspiration.

Liam looks at Madi.

Madi looks at Liam.

"I think it is time, Liam," Madi cries.

Liam is up and dressed. He helps Madi put something comfortable on to travel. She has a bag packed at the front door. She knew this day would come. Liam starts the car to let it warm up. He puts the bag in the backseat. They have a little time but only God knows.

"Please pray," Madi says.

Liam holds her hand and bows his head.

Heavenly Father

Thank you for all you have given us.
Bless this house and this baby, and Madi, too.
Bring us home healthy and safely.

Amen

Liam helps Madi into the car. He heads down the road to the hospital. The doctor assured them everything is normal. Madi is having contractions. Liam knows nothing about babies. He wants to get Madi into care soon.

He arrives at the hospital. The parking lot is full. He parks the car nearby on the street.

"Are you ok, to walk, Madi?" Liam asks.

"I can drop you off at the door," he says. He turns around and pulls her up to the emergency doors.

He helps her from the car.

"Wait inside," he says. "I will park the car and be right back."

"Thank you, Liam," Madi says. "See you, soon."

Madi checks in.

Liam parks the car. He grabs her bag and runs the distance to the doors. He finds Madi sitting and stable.

"I am going in soon," Madi says. "It is time."

It is not long before Liam is holding his newborn son in his arms. Liam hands him to Madi, gently placing him in her arms.

Madi smiles. She is going to need rest.

Seth Liam Nam was born the morning of February twenty-second, six and a half pounds strong.

Liam cries.

Madi cries.

Liam prays

Heavenly Father

Thank you for this beautiful healthy baby boy, this loan from you
Help us to raise him for you
Bless us with life in you forevermore

Amen

Thirty-Nine

Madi and Liam arrive home with the new baby, the next day. He is happy and healthy.

The nursery has been prepared ahead of time. Liam has tidied the house for their homecoming. He wants Madi to rest as much as possible when she gets home. She has her work cut out for her.

Liam unlocks the front door. The baby wrapped tight in his seat. He pulls the seat from the car and carries him inside. He is anxious to get him out of the cold. He returns to help Madi from the car.

Madi is happy to be home. She cannot wait to sleep in her own bed, tonight. She prays she can sleep.

Madi wants to nurse and give the baby the nutrients he needs for a good start as God intended for him.

Madi and Liam put their boots and coats aside.

Madi tends to little Seth. He is beginning to stir. He opens his eyes to see his new world. They look at Seth and at each other.

Madi smiles at her son.

"We made it this far," Liam says. "The first addition of our little family." Madi smiles.

Madi is happy to be home.

"It is soon time to establish new rules for this family," Liam says.

"Yes, I believe so," Madi replies. "Life is going to be different."

"Did you call my parents?" Madi asks.

"Not yet," Liam replies. "I thought I would wait until we were all home."

"Thank you," Madi says. "I will take Seth from his seat."

"We should do it soon." she says.

Madi sits on the sofa with Seth in her arms.

Liam joins her carrying his telephone.

"Are you ready?" Liam asks.

"Yes," Madi replies, "before he wakes."

Liam dials the number.

"Hello, Liam," Elisabeth answers.

"Is everything well?" he asks.

"We would like you to come by the house and meet your grandson, Seth Liam," Liam says.

Elisabeth is quiet. She calls for Steven to join her.

"What time do you want us to come by?" Elisabeth asks.

"Tomorrow after lunch is fine," Liam replies.

Liam looks at Madi.

"Are you well, Madi?" Elisabeth asks.

"Very well," Madi replies. "Now I am home."

"We are happy to hear," Elisabeth replies for both her and Steven.

Madi's father rarely speaks up for himself. He finds it easier to let Elisabeth do the talking.

It is their business.

Liam is thankful Madi allows him time to speak.

Madi knows Liam well. She respects him.

Madi's parents knock at the front door the next day. She greets them with a smile and a hug. Brent is with them, too. She takes their coats and sets them all aside. They put their boots against the wall. Madi leads them to the front room where baby Seth is in his seat. They are grateful he is awake. They can see his eyes and his lips. *"Is it a smile, we do not really know but God does?"*

Madi and Liam work hard to maintain a respectful relationship. Madi is happy to have Liam at home. He will have to go back to work soon. She is accepting their respective roles in the home and at work. She has her handfuls now.

Madi needs Liam more, now, and Liam the same. Madi loves her role in the home as the mother. The discipline and rules she will leave in Liam's hands. It is better that way.

Forty

Liam wakes the next morning at six o'clock. He needs to get back to the diner. He has so much to catch up. Doris will be anxious to hear the news. Liam knows Doris is going to want to stop by the house. He is surprised she did not call.

Liam arrives at the diner at eight o'clock to open the doors.

Today is Tuesday. It will not be too busy.

Doris greets him at the front door with a smile.

"Congratulations, little brother," she says. "I cannot wait to meet the little guy."

"Thank you, sis," Liam replies.

"He is something," Liam says. "We named him Seth Liam."

"Very nice!" she says. "Maybe I can stop by the house Friday, after work."

"That will be fine," Liam replies. "I will let Madi know to expect you."

"I need to get something done," he says walking towards the office.

131

"This side of the fort is mine for a while," Liam says. "I want Madi at home."

"It is what we agree is best for the house," Liam says.

"That is a good idea," Doris replies.

"Being her first and all," Doris speaks. "She has some learning to do."

"Is she part of a community group or a church."

Liam looks at his sister, "I think you know Madi almost as much as I do."

"No, we are fine for now," Liam replies.

"If she needs support," Liam says. "We will find it."

"Good for you," Doris replies. Doris got the hint to mind her own business. She is comfortable the two of them will be fine. She let Liam go back to his business.

Business at the diner is not the same without Madi. Liam misses her smile and sunny disposition around the customers. Her customers miss her, too. They often ask about her and the baby. Liam promises when the weather warms up, he will bring them out to the diner. Becky is up to speed on the tasks. She is good at what she does, too. She is not Madi. Liam knows he is going to have to adapt to the new way of life.

Liam cannot wait to get home at the end of the day. He likes the way she surprises him with a new dinner entrée or the décor in a certain room. The chatter over tea because she, too, misses the social life of the diner. Babies are lovely but they are not much of a social life at this stage. Liam looks forward to the day Madi returns to the diner. He will leave it up to her.

Madi keeps the house tidy, and the laundry done. Dinner is on the table when he arrives. When dinner is not prepared there is a note on the fridge to order in. And sometimes there is a telephone message to pick up dinner on the way home.

Madi never misses a beat. She keeps up the home.

Liam does the lawn or shovels the snow in the morning or the evening. If he cannot get to it, Madi picks it up.

This is normal stuff in the balance of life, work, and play.

As Seth grows and the weather warms, they will find their way back into the outdoor world. They will walk along the river and go to parks. They will chase the geese and listen to the birds and rabbits, too. They will have backyard BBQ's and build a tree house. They will watch the cloud formations in the day sky and stargaze on the warmer nights.

About the author

Candace C Wells

I grew up near the Rocky Mountains in Alberta, Canada.
I learned to love the rivers, mountains, and valleys of both
Alberta and British Columbia, Canada. I grew up in a blessed
and beautiful land. I traveled the Western provinces and
Northwestern USA as a young person. I migrated to the city
life to find employment and I maintain lifestyle, as such.
My desire is to find my way back to the quietness of the open
land one day. I enjoy the beauty of nature and all of God's
creation. I am a Christian and have walked with God most of my
days. I have faltered along the way ever reaching out for God
and his infinite grace and mercies in my time of need. There is
no place to far our God cannot see or find us. All of you that
read my books –I write to share the love of God, peace, and
joy that comes in knowing he does genuinely love us.

*For God so loved the world, that he gave his only begotten
Son, that whosoever believeth in him should not perish but
have everlasting life. John 3:16 KJV*